Break Point

Rosie Rushton lives in Northamptonshire. She took up writing because it gave her a wonderful excuse not to do the dusting and because the word processor was the only thing in the house that didn't answer back. Her three daughters managed to attain adulthood despite having the most embarrassing mother in Northamptonshire. She is passionately interested in family and relationship issues. In addition to writing teenage fiction and running workshops in schools around the country, Rosie is training to be a Reader in the Church of England. After having her first TV mini series, *Zone Two*, shown on BBC 2 in 1999, Rosie's ambitions are to write full-length dramas for teenage audiences and to have her adult novel published before she is too old to look good in the publicity photographs.

Other books by Rosie Rushton, published by Piccadilly Press:

FICTION

In the Best Friends series:
Best Friends – Together
Best Friends – Getting Sorted
Best Friends – In Love

In The Girls series:
Poppy ★ Olivia ★ Sophie ★
Melissa ★ Jessica

In The Leehampton Quartet:
Just Don't Make a Scene, Mum! ★
I Think I'll Just Curl Up and Die
How Could You Do This To Me, Mum?
Where Do We Go From Here?

PS He's Mine!
(co-authored with Nina Schindler)
Tell Me I'm OK, Really

NON-FICTION

Speak for Yourself
Staying Cool,
Surviving School
You're My Best Friend,
I Hate You!

Break Point

ROSIE RUSHTON

PICCADILLY PRESS • LONDON

My grateful thanks go to Steve Herr, Bob Herr, George Lippi and all those members of 381st BGMA stationed in England during the Second World War, who were so generous with their advice on Zack's experiences; to Lucinda Armstrong and Anna Hodgkinson for keeping me up to date with today's teen scene; and to my many friends whose memories of being young in the sixties were somewhat more adventurous than my own.

First published in Great Britain in 2002
by Piccadilly Press Ltd.,
5 Castle Road, London NW1 8PR

A catalogue record for this book is available
from the British Library

ISBNs: 1 85340 770 4 (trade paperback)
1 85340 775 5 (hardback)

3 5 7 9 10 8 6 4 2

Printed and bound in Great Britain by Bookmarque Ltd.

Design by Judith Robertson
Cover design by Fielding Design Ltd

Set in 11.5pt Bembo and Trajan

EMILY

June

I'M A LIAR.

A hypocrite and a liar. Of course, no one else knows that – least of all, any of these people crowding around me now. To them, I'm just Emily Driver, aged sixteen-and-a-half, straight sets winner of the Under 18s East Sussex Tennis Championship. It's hardly Wimbledon; but the seaside daily papers are out in force.

'Look this way, Emily! Smile!'

I incline my head towards yet another camera and beam broadly.

'Hold the cup a bit higher, Emily!'

My arms obediently stretch themselves skywards and the sun glints off the silver trophy. I am conscious of my damp pony tail and the perspiration trickling down the back of my neck – all I want to do is escape to have a shower.

'How does it feel to be the champion, Emily?' A bearded man in a revolting orange shirt with the words HOT FM blazoned across it thrusts a microphone under my nose.

'Brilliant!' I reply brightly, edging nearer the club house door. 'Really cool!' I say that every time. It used to be true.

'That's three in a row, isn't it, Emily?' shouts another. 'So what next?'

Careful. Don't commit yourself.

'European circuit, Emily? Is that it?'

Say nothing. Just wave and walk away.

'Thanks, everyone. Thanks a lot.' I turn decisively and walk towards the changing room. I'm pretty amazed that my mother hasn't appeared. She left the stands the moment I hit that winning backhand and she doesn't usually miss the chance to do the supportive mother bit in the background of every photograph.

'Come on, Emily! What are your plans?' The small clutch of press people are following hard on my heels. I have a sudden urge to turn and shout at them.

What does it matter what my plans are? I want to yell. What makes any of you think that my plans have anything to do with what happens in my life? But of course, I don't.

'Just to keep on doing my best!' I reply, hating myself for the sugary response, but hoping it will shut them up.

It does. A couple more camera flashes and the pack start drifting away.

'Emily!' An urgent voice calls my name but this time I'm ignoring it. Enough is enough. I want to catch up with Mia, make sure she's not too stressed out because I beat her. It's hard when you have to play against someone you really like. And if I hurry, I can still be home in time to get to Viki's party.

'Emily, wait. Please!'

I'm about to push open the changing room door when

a hand shoots out from nowhere and grabs the handle, barring my way.

'What?' I spin around and find myself eyeball-to-eyeball with a very red-faced guy with the most enormous grey eyes.

'Sorry – really, I *am* sorry,' he gasps, 'only I forgot to put a cassette in my tape recorder and I hardly got anything down on paper because my pen ran out and I only started at the *Argus* four weeks ago and if I go back to the editor and say . . .'

I'm tired. I don't want to talk to anyone else about tennis or the future or how I managed to improve my net game this summer. I want to go home.

For once, I wish my mother was on hand to rescue me.

'I'm sorry,' I begin, 'I really have to –'

'What you really have to do is talk to me,' he finishes for me. 'Just for a minute. It could make all the difference to . . .'

'Look, Mr . . .' Why I'm calling him Mr anything, heaven knows. He doesn't look much older than me. But I have to say something.

'Hugo. Hugo Fraser,' he says sticking out his hand. I shake it. It's hot and sticky and I have an urge to wipe my hand on my tennis dress. '*Evening Argus* reporter. Well, trainee actually.' He sighs. 'It's part of my college course – secondment to a newspaper for six months to "prove myself".'

'Well, I . . .' I really don't have time for all this.

'The thing is, if I don't get some decent copy from you within the next five minutes my editor is going to write an awful report back to college.' He gives a wry grin and looks at me pleadingly. 'Give me a break – please.'

A strand of ridiculously blond hair flops in his eye. He really is quite cute when he smiles.

'OK, then,' I sigh. I don't want to hang about but I know what it's like to have someone hounding you all the time. 'But it will have to be quick. What do you want to know?'

'Something new, something different, something about the off-court Emily!' Suddenly he's fired up, eager, pen poised over the notebook he has whipped out of his jacket pocket. 'I mean, is there anything in your life except tennis?'

'I wish!' The words are out before I know it. 'I mean, I wish I could tell you what tennis means to me . . .' I stammer; but I can see that Hugo isn't taken in.

'Pressure, eh?' he chips in at once. 'That would make a good piece, particularly if . . .'

'Emily, darling! There you are!' The changing room door has just swung open, nearly knocking both of us off our feet.

'Emily, you've done it!' My mother springs forward, grabs the trophy from my hands and envelopes me in a hug. 'Well played, darling! I knew you could do it!'

This isn't strictly true, because after my semifinal, which I only just managed to win on a tie-break, she nagged me for hours about my lack of concentration and how I was about to let the opportunity of a lifetime slip through my fingers.

'Now hurry up, sweetheart!' she urges, pulling me

through the door. 'You can change later – you've got to go upstairs to the players' lounge now!' She winks at me and my heart sinks. I don't have to be a genius to work out the reason for her excitement. It's exactly what I've been dreading.

'Emily, if I could just ask you a couple of questions about . . .' Hugo touches my arm.

'I'm sorry!' My mother spots his press badge and leaps forward like a lioness protecting a newborn cub. 'She's not talking to the press any more today!'

She goes to shut the door but Hugo's foot is firmly in the way. Clearly, he's met mothers like mine before.

'OK,' I say, more to irritate my mother than because I want to, 'fire away!'

'Emily, there's no time!' My mother grabs my arm. 'Felix is waiting!' She hisses the last three words under her breath.

My heart sinks. I was right.

Mum pulls me into the changing room. Hugo makes a valiant attempt to follow.

'Felix? Would that be . . .' But my mother has slammed the door firmly shut.

'Listen, Emily,' she gabbles, shoving me up the stairs ahead of her, 'I can't be sure, of course, but I think he's going to do what we hoped.'

What *you* hoped, I want to say – but of course, I don't.

'It won't take long, will it?' I mutter instead. 'I've got to get home and change and be at Viki's by . . .'

'Oh, for goodness' sake, Emily! What does a party matter compared with this?' my mother demands.

And that just about sums it up. Mum only ever sees me as Emily, the tennis hopeful. What's more, she expects me to think of myself that way too. All the time.

I can't really blame her; I used to be mad about the sport myself. But these days, it's not enough. The trouble is, no one seems to understand.

Last month, for example, I was feeling really uptight and knotted inside – I hate having to make decisions at the best of times – and my best mate Charlie kept asking what was wrong, so I tried to tell her.

'It's just that everything is so difficult right now,' I said. OK, so maybe I could have put it better given time but that's how it came out. Of course, Charlie just fell about.

'Difficult? Get real, Emily!' she groaned. 'You've got it made! You don't know how lucky you are.'

Charlie is starting to sound more like my mother every day, which is worrying in someone of sixteen. To be fair, though, she does have one quality that my mother lacks: she occasionally tries to see things from my point of view.

'I mean,' she went on hurriedly, 'I know how hard you have to practise for all those matches and everything – and I guess it was pretty awful having to miss Abby's all-night party . . .'

I didn't just miss Abby's party, but the opening of the FlyHi club, and Jemma's barbecue, and half a dozen other fun things over the past few months. My social life is the pits. Correction: my social life is non-existent. But right now it's my future that's worrying me more.

'But,' Charlie continued, 'you *do* keep winning cups and

getting your picture in the papers – and at least you don't have to sit through boring Careers Evenings and worry about what you are going to do with your life. You've got it sussed.'

I didn't argue at the time. I would have done, but we were in Physics, and Mrs Jessop's neck was turning red, which is always a prelude to one of her 'You weren't put on this earth to chat!' lectures. And besides, I was pretty sure that if I said any more, I would cry, and I couldn't risk that happening. People don't expect you to cry when you've just been called '*the hope on Britain's tennis horizon*' by a national newspaper.

My mother loved that. I'm not saying that I wasn't chuffed, because I was – you can't help enjoying it when people make a fuss over you – but Mum went totally over the top. Not that she needed any encouragement. Ever since I was about ten, she's had this idea in her head that I'm going to become a superstar and win Wimbledon and the US Open and all the other big tournaments.

'You can do it, Emily, I know you can!' she says a dozen times a week. 'Just a bit more effort and a few more hours a week in training . . .'

What she won't understand is that I don't have any more effort and I don't have any more hours. And if I did, I don't think I'd want to spend them on a tennis court.

It's awful when the thing you've put all your energy into for years finally happens, and you find you want something else. And if Felix Fordyce is about to offer me what my mother thinks he is – then I'm just going to have to come clean and face the consequences. I'll have to tell them both straight: There's more to life than tennis.

'Now Emily, be polite, be enthusiastic, be modest – but not too modest – I mean, we want him to see that you have faith in your own abilities and . . .' Mum is in full flood as we reach the door to the players' lounge.

'Felix is going to offer you a place at his Academy, I just know he is!' She is so excited that she can hardly get the words out. 'Oh darling, won't it be wonderful?'

I look at her. She actually has tears in her eyes as she pats her hair into place and straightens her shoulders. I smile and nod. 'Fantastic!' I hear myself say.

Like I said, I'm a liar.

I don't get it. I wish I understood myself. I mean, this is what I've been working towards for the past eight years. Most of the girls on the circuit would kill to be in my shoes right now. Come to think of it, some of the bitchier ones will probably have a pretty good go at it when they hear the news.

'So get this, Emmy-lee,' Felix begins in that Southern drawl of his, rocking on his heels and gazing out of the window at the deserted courts, 'I want y'all to realise that what I'm offering you ain't no easy ticket, kiddo. You're good – you're damn good!'

Mum pokes me in the back.

'Thank you,' I whisper obediently.

'But you ain't good enough yet!' he retorts. 'Not by a long chalk. And if I'm gonna make you a star, I want total, utter, complete dedication – get it?'

I nod. I don't dare speak. I'm afraid that if I open my mouth I'll cry, and crying in front of the top coach in England wouldn't go down at all well.

'From now on, you won't talk to the press unless I'm with you, you won't drink, and you certainly won't burn the candle at both ends – OK?'

'Of course!' my mother chirps brightly, but then she's not the one having her entire life put on hold.

'There will be times you'll hate me!' Felix cries, grinning from ear to ear as if the prospect of my loathing really excites him. 'There will be times you'll wish I'd never left Louisiana!'

My mother titters politely behind me. I don't like to tell the guy I'm wishing that already.

It's crazy. If this had happened a year ago, I would have been over the moon. Twelve months ago, all I wanted out of life was to be the best tennis player the world has ever seen, another Martina Hingis, Venus Williams, Jennifer Capriati. A year ago, I was just another fifteen-year-old kid with outsize dreams and tunnel vision. Now, I'm sixteen with my feet on the ground, a different dream – and one hell of a mess to get myself out of.

'Emily won't let you down, Felix!' My mother has gone all pink and dewy-eyed. 'This is a dream come true for her, isn't it darling?'

I know that this is the moment for me to speak, to tell

them what I really want to do – but I can't. My mouth has gone dry and it feels as if there is a huge pebble stuck in my throat.

Luckily, Felix hasn't finished. 'Now, about the money side of things,' he begins. 'My Tennis Academy doesn't come cheap, even with the scholarship I'm offering Emmy-lee. That only covers the coaching – then there's the boarding fee, the tournament fees, travel expenses . . .'

A great surge of relief floods through my body and I can actually feel my shoulders relax. We can't possibly afford it – Mum is forever going on about the cost of new racquets and tennis lessons, not to mention all the petrol it takes to get to the tournaments, and my tennis shoes. It's not that we're hard up, exactly, but ever since Dad left years ago to (in his words) find himself in South America, Mum's worried herself sick about the finances.

I turn to Mum to reassure her that it's OK, that I won't be disappointed when she has to say no. To my surprise, Mum is grinning from ear to ear.

'Not a problem,' she announces, waving her hand weakly in Felix's face. 'We're prepared to sacrifice whatever it takes, aren't we, Emmy?'

No! I want to scream. You may be, but I'm not. Not any more. Not for this!

So why is my head nodding up and down?

You're crazy! I want to shout at her – there isn't anything else to give up. We've already stopped having holidays, stopped decorating the house, stopped doing anything that isn't related to tennis. I don't want to live like this any more!

Those are the things I want to say. So why am I smiling meekly at Felix, and shaking his hand and thanking him for his trust in me? Why, in short, am I such a total and complete wimp?

❧

My mother has finally stopped talking. Mind you, it's taken the whole of the journey from Eastbourne to Hove for her to shut up. Sadly, it only took the first half mile for the last faint glimmer of hope at the back of my mind to be shattered.

'Mum?' I ventured, as she manoeuvred the car through the gates of Devonshire Park and out on to the main road. 'I know it's very exciting about this scholarship and everything but –'

'It's wonderful, isn't it, darling?' she interrupted. 'This could be the making of you, Emily. All those years of scrimping and saving to pay for lessons . . .'

I grabbed at the opportunity. 'That's just it, Mum!' I gabbled. 'I mean, you heard what Felix said about how expensive it's all going to be. I don't want you to keep spending money on me and I honestly don't mind if –'

'Darling, it's sweet of you!' she cried. 'But it's all going to be just fine! I had a most amazing brainwave.' She turned to watch my reaction and the car swerved dangerously into the middle of the road.

'Mum!' I grabbed the dashboard as she steered back on course.

'Oh, whoops!' she said cheerfully, ignoring the rather rude hand gesture from an oncoming motorist. 'It came to me last week but I didn't say anything until I'd discussed it with Lally.'

'Lally?' I gasped. (I should explain that Lally is my grandmother – when I was tiny and heard people calling her Alice, all I could manage was Lally. And it stuck. She's great but there is no way I could imagine my mother having a rational discussion with her on anything. It's not that they don't get on, exactly; it's just that whenever she comes to visit us, most of their conversations run along the lines of 'Oh mother, why can't you act your age!' and 'Ruth, loosen up, dear!' followed by a lot of meaningful sniffing and loud door slamming.)

'What has Lally got to do with it?' I asked.

'We,' my mother announced, pulling up at the traffic lights and turning to face me, 'are going to sell up. We're going to move in with your grandmother.'

'WHAT?' She had to be joking. I mean, we've got a perfectly good house of our own. Well, OK, not perfectly good, but adequate. It was perfectly awful when we bought it, but Mum's really arty. People even pay good money to get her to paint murals for their kids' bedrooms. After she stopped teaching, she started painting murals as a hobby. Now our house is quite funky, if you overlook the windows that don't fit properly and the boiler that clanks half the night.

'We can't move in with Lally!' I gasped. I mean, I love my grandmother dearly, largely because she is totally off the wall and not a bit grandmotherly; but she is certainly not the sort of woman you want to live with if you are planning to remain sane for the foreseeable future.

'Of course we can!' Mum declared, just a shade less confidently. 'After all, it's far too big for her on her own. I sell our place, invest the money, and that pays for all your coaching and . . .'

'Mum, no!' I protested. This was all going too far, too fast. I can't let her do this.

'What do you mean, no?' she challenged me. 'Last week, you said you wished we had a bit more spare cash. This way – we will have!' She beamed at me triumphantly.

'Lally's very excited about it,' she gabbled on. 'She's going to clear out those two attic rooms and make them yours, darling, and best of all, I'm getting the conservatory as a studio. So at last, I'll be able to . . .'

Whether it was post-match exhaustion or guilt about what I knew I had to tell her, or anger at being too pathetic to get on and do it, I'm not sure, but something inside me snapped.

'Mum, you're being ridiculous! I don't want her attic, thank you – and besides, we can't just up and move house!'

'Why not?' she demanded. 'People do it all the time.' Very witty.

'That's not the point!' I retaliated. 'What about school? I don't want to travel right across town every . . .'

The moment I had said the words, I knew what was coming next.

Mum laughed 'Silly! You won't be at Trinity High any

more, will you? You'll be boarding at the Tennis Academy.'

That's when it hit me. I still can't get my head around it. This is for real. By September, my whole life will have changed. I'll be miles away in Surrey; I won't see my friends and I won't be going into the Sixth Form.

And if I don't go into the Sixth Form, all my dreams . . .

I bite my lip. I can feel the tears welling up. 'How could you do this, Mum?' I burst out. 'How could you go ahead with all these plans and not even mention them to me?'

OK, so I know I haven't told Mum what I've been planning, but that's different. I haven't quite found the words yet.

Mum waves a hand dismissively. 'Well, I didn't want to raise your hopes – not until Felix had made a firm offer!' She smiles. 'But now that he's agreed to take you on, it's full steam ahead! The house is going on the market first thing on Monday morning!'

She turns to me and squeezes my knee. 'I'm so proud of you, sweetheart,' she says. 'Today you made it all worthwhile. All those years of driving you to training sessions, going without holidays, staying in those grotty B&Bs at tournaments!' She sighs happily. 'And now, with Felix behind you, anything could happen!'

I can feel the tears pricking behind my eyes. Mum might find it all terribly exciting, but I know exactly what will happen – an even more punishing schedule of practice, practice, practice. No parties, hardly any time to get my homework done, every weekend taken up with tournaments. I don't want to do it. I can't do it. Thinking about it is making my heart race.

'Listen, Mum, there's something I want to say . . .' I begin.

'Darling, isn't that your phone?'

A muffled *bleep* emanates from my sports bag.

'Hurry up,' my mother urges impatiently as I lean over to the back seat and wrestle with the bag. 'It might be Felix – he said he'd ring with dates and stuff.'

It isn't Felix. It's Charlie.

'Hi, Em! Listen, this is so amazing! Guess who is going to be at Viki's party tonight? You will die!'

'Who?' I ask, my mind still lurching between the thought of living in my grandmother's attic and facing Felix across a tennis net five times a week.

'Rufus!' Charlie cries. 'So what do you say to that?'

Despite everything, my heart leaps.

'Really?' I gasp. 'At Viki's? Tonight?'

Charlie bursts out laughing.

'I thought that would get you going,' she says giggling. 'He got back from wherever it was he went . . .'

'Borneo,' I interject. Viki's brother, who is the most gorgeous guy in the universe, is on a gap year. Sadly, he chose to spend it about as far away from here as he could manage. And anyway, he rarely notices my existence.

'Who? What about Borneo?' My mother, who has ears like a bat's radar, frowns at me.

I give her a withering look as Charlie chats on.

'. . . Well, he got back a couple of days ago and now the party's going to be a sort of joint seventeenth for Viki and welcome home for him. And you know what that means?'

'What?'

My mother has now started her finger-tapping routine – the one she always employs if I'm on my mobile for more than half a millisecond. She thinks I'll fry my brain.

'Boys, silly – he'll be inviting loads of his mates. The place will be overrun with proper men.'

Despite myself, I giggle. 'Hardly men – he's only nineteen, silly,' I remind her.

Charlie sighs loudly. 'Emily, that remark shows how little you know about guys. Anyway, tonight is your big chance. You can't stay celibate for ever, tennis or no tennis. What are you wearing?'

My mind begins racing through my wardrobe, which doesn't take long because I must be the most garment-challenged girl in my entire year. When you live three quarters of your life in tracksuits and tennis shorts, you tend to get a bit behind in the fashion stakes.

'I don't know,' I mumble.

'Don't know what?' my mother asks. She is so nosy.

'Wear the black trousers and that silk camisole thing,' orders Charlie, without waiting for me to answer. 'Show off those amazing boobs!'

Charlie has a thing about my chest but then she doesn't have to live with it bouncing up and down all the time like a couple of unrestrained Swiss rolls. Thank heaven for sports bras.

'See you there, then!' she goes on. 'Oh, and by the way – did you do what I said? This afternoon, I mean?'

'Not exactly,' I confess. I haven't allowed myself to dwell on what Charlie would think about my 6–3, 6–4 win – not after our conversation last Thursday.

'Oh Emily!' she sighs. 'You didn't go and win again, did you?'

'Mmmm,' I murmur.

'But we agreed . . .' she begins, and then sighs. 'Oh well, just don't moan to me that your life's in a mess, will you? See ya!'

And with that, the phone goes dead.

'I assume that was Charlotte?' my mother asks. She's the only person in the universe who calls Charlie by her full name. 'Why didn't you tell her your good news?'

'We were talking about the party,' I snap. 'There are other things in life, you know!'

My mother raises an eyebrow.

'Not for much longer,' she says. 'You know what Felix said about partying and wild living . . .'

I close my eyes. There's about as much chance of me getting a taste of wild living as there is of Rufus Dean falling madly in love with me.

Mum isn't speaking now. She thinks I'm asleep but I'm not. I'm thinking about Charlie and everything she's been saying to me for the last month.

'If you don't want this Felix person to pick you for his tennis school, start losing your matches!' she told me. 'It's not rocket science, Em! Play badly this season – assuming you know how. If you're not winning, he won't want you.'

And that's what I had meant to do with this tournament. Well, not to start with, obviously. It would have looked a bit odd if I had lost the first round and anyway, the girl I was playing against was useless. I planned to fluff it in the semi-finals – and I nearly did. Except that when I was 1–4 down in the final set, it was as if someone had flicked a switch and the old me was back on court. Suddenly, I just knew I had to win – not because I wanted to, because something inside was driving me to. And of course, once I'd hit a couple of ace forehands and won my next serve game, that was it. The adrenalin was pumping and the determination to slam my opponent into the middle of tomorrow fortnight took over.

I don't know why that happens. I wish it didn't. When I'm on the court, I want to win. It's just that once I'm off the court, I don't want to take the consequences of victory.

I'm a mess.

'What on earth is *she* doing here?'

My mother's voice snaps me out of my reverie and my eyes jerk open.

Standing on the pavement outside our house is my grandmother. There can't be many 75-year-olds who are happy to stand in the street wearing a brown fringed suede skirt, knee-high boots, a checked shirt with a scarf knotted at the neck and a stetson that appears to be two sizes too big. But then, there aren't many 75-year-olds like Lally.

'Well, howdee folks!' she cries as the car pulls up. Lally

is into all things American. Every year she goes to the States, a different part every time. Last time it was Montana, which accounts for her current cowgirl phase.

'Yippee!' she shouts, clicking her fingers in the air as we pull up. My mother flinches visibly and jerks the hand brake with unnecessary force.

'Darling!' Lally cries, flinging open the door and squashing me in a big hug. 'You did it! You won! Radio Brighton had the results! I'm so proud of you!'

'Thanks,' I manage, as the breath is squeezed out of me.

'And Felix offered her a place at the Academy!' My mother slams the car door shut. 'Isn't that wonderful news?'

'Stunning!' Lally grabs my hand and drags me towards the front door. 'I'm so sorry I wasn't there to watch, sweetheart, but a bunch of us from the line dancing class were showing off our stuff at the Hospital Fête!'

She beams broadly and I try hard not to laugh.

'We raised a hundred and thirty-five pounds in forty minutes,' she adds proudly.

'People paying you to stop, were they?' Mum asks acerbically as she grapples the front door key. She thinks Lally should grow old gracefully.

'I shall ignore that remark,' Lally replies loftily. 'Now, Emmy love, did your mother tell you about our little plan?'

'Moving in with you?' I hesitate, playing for time.

Lally nods eagerly. 'What do you think of that?'

'I don't know . . .' I stammer, dumping my tennis bag on the floor.

'I knew you'd love it!' Lally slaps her thigh and looks as

if she is about to burst into a quick chorus of 'Oklahoma!'. 'It will make things so much easier all round.'

I can't quite see how. After all, Mum disapproves of almost everything that Lally gets up to, and Lally spends her life telling Mum that she is too uptight and should live for the moment. So then Mum shouts and says that it's a bit late for that, and Lally says you shouldn't keep throwing the past back in people's faces, and then one of them storms out whichever house they are in at the time and goes back home.

Which will be fun when there's nowhere else for either of them to go.

'Mother, what *are* you doing here?' Mum asks as Lally strides down the hallway ahead of her. 'We agreed that Emily and I would come over for lunch tomorrow . . .'

Oh great. Organising my life again. The one day I don't have to be on a tennis court and my mother decides to fill it up.

'Yes, I know all that!' Lally chirps. 'But you will never guess what I've done this afternoon!'

'Aside from making a spectacle of yourself, you mean?' my mothers mutters under her breath, plugging in the kettle. She kicks off her shoes under the kitchen table.

'Aside from having a whole bunch of fun!' retorts Lally. 'Although, of course, you wouldn't understand that concept, would you dear?'

Honestly, they've only been together for five minutes and they are at it already. No way can they live together. No way can *I* stand the strain.

'I'm off to get changed,' I announce.

'Changed? What for?' demands Mum, hurling tea bags into the pot.

'The party,' I say as patiently as I can. 'Tonight. At Viki's. Remember?' It's like addressing a small child.

'Oh, yes,' she sighs. 'I suppose this means I've got to turn out again to ferry you over there?'

'You promised . . .'

'I'll take you, darling!' interrupts Lally. 'I'm in no hurry.'

'Mother, don't be ridiculous!' Mum interjects, unplugging the kettle. 'You can't possibly do that!'

For once, I'm with my mother one hundred per cent.

'I thought she needed a lift,' says Lally, frowning.

'Not,' stresses my mother, 'in that clapped-out heap of a rust bucket, thank you very much. You might be prepared to take your life into your hands every day, but leave Emily out of it.'

I sigh with relief. It's not that arriving at a party in your grandmother's bright orange Chevrolet is the problem; most of my mates thinks she dead cool in a 'thank heavens she's no relation of mine' kind of way. But Lally's grasp of the Highway Code leaves a lot to be desired, and she has a habit of making rude gestures at anyone who takes up what she thinks of as her space. It's very embarrassing.

'I suppose I'll have to take you.' Mum pours the tea and slumps down in the nearest chair.

Oh good. Pity she couldn't have said that to start with. I grab a biscuit and make for the door.

'So, as I was saying,' Lally begins. 'This afternoon, I

actually managed to . . . Oh, no!' She jumps to her feet and begins looking wildly round the room.

'What now?' sighs my mother.

'My bracelet!' Lally stares at her wrist in disbelief. 'It's gone.'

'Your shilling one?' Mum asks.

'Of course my shilling one!' cries Lally. 'The one I always wear. I can't bear it!'

To be honest, the bracelet isn't even that pretty – just an old silver coin from way back on a rather ugly chain. But Lally's worn it ever since I can remember and it's got this dead sad story that goes with it.

'Don't worry, it can't have gone,' my mother replies. 'Emily, have a look for it, will you?'

'Mum, it's seven o'clock! I'll be late and –'

Mum glares at me and jerks her head in Lally's direction. Lally's down on her hands and knees, searching under the table – and her hands are shaking.

'I'll look in the hall,' I say helpfully, glancing at the clock and abandoning all thoughts of a long soak in the bath.

It isn't in the hall, or on the path, or in the pocket of Lally's jacket. I even suggest she hunts in her car but that draws a blank too.

'I must go!' she stammers. 'I have to find it. I've had it since I was sixteen.' She actually has tears in her eyes. I try to think of something I've got now that is that important to me, but I can't.

'Maybe it fell off while you were at the Fête,' I suggest. 'You could phone the hospital and . . .'

'You're right! I'll go there now! I have to find it – I can't bear to not have it on my wrist!'

Mum puts an arm round her shoulder. 'It will turn up,' she says soothingly. 'Perhaps you forgot to put it on this morning or . . .'

'Don't be silly!' Lally snaps. 'I never take it off. Never!' She rams her arms into her cardigan and opens the front door. 'It's an omen, I know it is . . .'

'Oh, mother, don't be ridiculous!' Mum's gentle moment has clearly passed. 'An omen of what, for heaven's sake?'

'Oh, nothing.' Lally's shoulders slump and for a moment she looks like an old lady. 'I'll see you for lunch tomorrow.'

Mum shuts the front door with a sigh and turns to me. 'I do hope she finds it,' she says. 'It'll break her heart if it's really lost.'

I nod. Lally's mum died when Lally was my age but the saddest thing is that she was holding an envelope and on it were the words 'Alice's pocket money'. My grandfather soldered the coin on to a link bracelet and apparently she's never taken it off.

'So why did she say that losing it was an omen?' I ask. 'I mean, her mum's already dead and . . .'

Mum shrugs her shoulders. 'Don't ask me,' she murmurs. 'Old people get funny ideas in their heads sometimes.'

She glances at her watch. 'Hey, you'd better hurry up if I'm taking you to that party,' she says. 'And, by the way, I'll be there to fetch you at eleven o'clock sharp.'

'MUM!' I protest. 'That's far too early . . .'

'Eleven,' she repeats firmly. 'You need your sleep and . . .'

'I need a life,' I mutter back, but of course she ignores me.

'Besides, I know only too well what happens at these parties and the later it gets, the bigger the risks.'

If you ask me, it's not only old people that go funny in the head.

❧

'save me! mum says home @ 11.
can i spend nite w u? em'

I'm standing in my bra and knickers, zapping a text message to Charlie. I cannot believe that my mother expects me to come home so early – I'm sixteen, for heaven's sake. She doesn't think twice, of course, about yanking me out of bed at five-thirty in the morning to drive twenty miles for tennis practice before school – but when I get the chance to have a bit of fun, she's suddenly obsessed with how much sleep I need. Hypocritical or what?

I'm half in and half out of my black trousers when the phone bleeps.

'course u can. wld it help if my ma rang yrs?'

Ace!

'thnks! don't let yr ma mention times!'

I can't wait for this party. Of course seeing Rufus is part of it. Not that he'll take any notice of me. He treats me like a little sister anyway. But the best bit about tonight will be seeing all my mates and having a laugh. This is the first Saturday in weeks that I've been at home, never mind free to have a drink and forget all about backhands and volleys.

And it will probably be one of the last. By September . . .

No. I'm not going to think about it. I'll sort all that tomorrow. Live for the moment, that's what Charlie always says.

And tonight, that's just what I'm going to do.

'Now, only one drink, Emily – you hear me?'

'Yes, Mum.'

'And keep your eyes open for substances!'

'Yes, Mum.'

'People can spike drinks without you ever –'

'MUM!' This is getting silly. She talks as if I don't have a brain.

'I'll be fine,' I tell her as calmly as I can. 'I'm sixteen years old – I can take care of myself!'

'That's what everyone thinks at your age,' she retorts. 'Until it's too late.'

My mother reads too many tabloids. I suppose she has to in order to make up for her own boring life.

'Bye, Mum!' I give her a big kiss and a hug.

'Have fun,' she says mournfully.

'I will!'

At least I know how to.

‘You,’ I tell Charlie, the moment we meet up at Viki’s house, ‘are a star!’

‘I know,’ she answers, grinning. ‘My mum told yours that you are such a good influence on me – that clinched it! Mind you, even my mother has her limitations. She’s coming for us at midnight, so we’d better get partying!’

To be honest – not that I would admit it to Charlie for one minute – I’m a bit nervous. It’s ages since I’ve been to a party – well, any of the ones given by my mates, that is. You can’t count end-of-tournament gatherings. For one thing, mothers and coaches and other boring people hang around, trying to outdo one another, and for another, the only people you get to talk to are the other players, and in my case I’ve beaten a lot of them and they ignore me like the plague. And after today, it can only get worse.

‘Hey, what’s with the worried expression?’ asks Charlie, grabbing my arm and dragging me into the kitchen to get a drink.

‘Felix offered me a place at the Academy,’ I mutter, perching myself on the edge of a huge pine table, ‘starting in September.’

‘Ah,’ says Charlie. ‘You said it was on the cards. And you don’t want to go?’

‘You *know* I don’t,’ I reply, raising my voice over the din of the music pumping out in the next room. ‘We’ve talked about it often enough.’

‘So, don’t go!’ Charlie shrugs. ‘It’s *your* life.’

She makes it all sound so simple.

'Mum seems to think . . .' I begin lamely.

'Your mother,' stresses Charlie, 'isn't the one being asked to put in fifteen hours of practice a week and give up fun, boys and alcohol! Speaking of which – drink?'

She waves a bottle of Bacardi in my face.

'Yeah, sure. Why not?' With the news I've had today I deserve a drink.

'Good!' She pours me a slug of Bacardi and tops it up with cola.

'Look,' she adds more gently, 'we'll talk about it later. Right now, it's party time!'

She shimmies off, waving her glass in the air and heading straight for a couple of tall guys, who are eyeing her up from the opposite side of the room.

'Hey, it's Emily! How are you doing, Tiddler?'

A firm hand clamps down on my shoulder and I don't have to turn around to know who it is. Rufus has called me Tiddler ever since he was eight and I was a very small, scrawny six-year-old. I didn't like it then, and I don't like it now.

But I adore him.

'Hi!' I murmur, trying to sound sophisticated and indifferent and failing miserably. 'How was Borneo?'

'Steamy and bug-ridden,' he says cheerfully. 'I had the best time!'

'Great!' I gulp down my drink to hide my embarrassment at not being able to think of anything more witty to say.

'And what about you?' he asks, and gestures to me to

hand over my glass so he can pour me another drink. 'Still bashing away at those balls?'

'Well, I . . .' I begin, but stop. Rufus is already looking over my shoulder at a group of guys pouring through the front door.

'Catch you later!' He heads off and I know he won't.

'Hey, Emily – over here!' Viki is waving frantically at me from the door to the garden. 'Quick!'

I push my way through the throng and something flashes in my eye.

'Got you!' exclaims Viki. 'Now take a look at this – cool or what?'

It's a digital camera – one of those really expensive ones that show you the picture on a little screen at the back.

'Dad gave it to me for my birthday,' she explains. 'And Mum gave me a scanner so I can do all my projects when I go to *college*!'

She stresses the word 'college', smiling smugly at the rest of us. Viki left school the day the GCSEs finished. She's going to do photography at college and wants to publish books full of arty in-your-face pictures – tramps lying in the gutter or kids scavenging on rubbish heaps in Brazil. When she told her parents that she wasn't staying on for A Levels, they didn't turn a hair; they just told her to follow her star and go find herself.

It must be good to have well-balanced parents. If I tell my mother that I actually *do* want to stay on for A Levels, she will go ballistic. And if I tell her what I want to do after that, she will tell me I'm mad.

Life is very unfair.

'So, did you win?' Anya asks, thrusting a bowl of peanuts under my nose. 'As if we didn't all know the answer.'

'Of course she won – and very easily!' The guy who speaks has just walked up behind Anya and looks vaguely familiar.

'Straight sets, 6–3, 6–4!' he continues. 'Five aces, and she never lost a service game!'

Anya, who for some reason has turned bright pink and dropped a handful of peanuts all over the carpet, looks at him wide-eyed.

'How do you know all that?'

'I was there!' he boasts, and that's when it clicks. It's that reporter guy – the one who was all flustered and confused. He doesn't look either flustered or confused now – in fact, he looks pretty cool.

'Mind you,' he carries on, turning to Anya, 'that's about all I know.'

He looks back at me. 'I reckon you owe me at least ten minutes' undivided attention,' he says. 'Just to make up for shunning me after the match!'

Oh, no – no way.

'I don't want to talk about –'

'I'll just get a drink and I'll be back!' With that he's off, dodging the dancers to get over to the drinks bar. He really does have a very cute bum.

'You never said you were friends with Hugo!' The look that Anya gives me is hardly overflowing with warmth.

'I'm not friends with him!' I protest. 'I'd never set eyes

on him until today and I . . .'

'So what's with the "undivided attention" bit then?' she retorts. 'Has he been trying it on or . . .'

'Anya, the only thing Hugo is trying to do is to get me to talk tennis for his wretched newspaper!' I interject. 'And right now, tennis is the last thing I want to think about.'

'In which case, you'd better make your escape,' warns Viki, grinning. 'He's coming back!'

'I'll keep him out of your way!' Anya doesn't wait for a reply and marches straight up to Hugo, removes his drink and begins dancing with him.

I turn to Viki and laugh. 'Something tells me she fancies him!'

'Emily,' she replies, 'show me one person of the male gender that Anya doesn't fancy! How's *your* love life, by the way?'

I say nothing.

'That good, eh?' She frowns. 'So what about all those dishy tennis-playing types you keep meeting?'

She doesn't get it. I don't have time to flirt, let alone build a relationship. The most I get to say to a guy at a tournament is 'Good luck', 'Well played' or 'Are you fixed up for the mixed doubles?' It's hardly the best seduction routine there is.

But I don't bother explaining all that to Viki. 'They're OK,' I tell her. 'But no one special.'

No one period.

I'm exhausted. I've been dancing for nearly three quarters of an hour. I even danced with Rufus for a few milliseconds until some leggy blonde in black leather came and dragged him off. Viki was snapping away with her camera and I think she took a close-up of us just as he kissed me. OK, so it was only a sort of peck on the cheek but it's more than he's ever done before. I think I'll ask her for a copy and pin it above my bed. Or not.

It's a brilliant party and I haven't had such a good time in ages although I rather think I might be just the tiniest bit lightheaded.

'You have been avoiding me!'

I spin round and suddenly I'm face-to-face with Hugo and he's thrusting a drink into my hands.

'That's right, I *have*!' I reply. I definitely am a little bit tipsy.

'Why?'

'Why? I'll tell you why – because I have no intention of mentioning the word *tennis* all evening. Get it?'

Hugo shrugs. 'Fine by me,' he says. 'To be honest, I find the whole sport thing rather boring.'

Oh, come on, pull the other one.

'So, if you don't like sport, how come you're a sports reporter?' I take a gulp of my drink and realise that actually I don't want any more. I feel a bit sick.

'I'm not – I was just filling in. Us trainees get to do anything and everything. The sports editor was covering the golf, the senior reporter is watching his wife give birth, the other two guys had to do the motor racing – and that left me. I'd never heard of you until yesterday!'

'Oh.' I feel really hot as well – and the room is wobbling rather alarmingly.

'Hang on – where are you going?' Hugo grabs my arm but I shake it off.

'I need some fresh air,' I mutter.

'I'll come with you,' he says, leading me towards the open French doors and grabbing a bottle of fizzy water on the way.

I would protest but I don't really want to risk opening my mouth.

'Emily!' I turn round and am almost blinded by a flash.

'Got you!' Viki gives me a huge wink and slips the camera strap over her head.

'Go for it, girl!' she mouths, giving me the thumbs-up sign.

Viki clearly thinks I'm about to snog Hugo, and I'm pretty sure I'm about to throw up.

'Sit!' demands Hugo as we reach a garden bench halfway up the vast lawn. 'Drink this!'

I take a few swigs from the bottle, have a very nasty few seconds and then begin to feel marginally better. There are couples dotted all over the garden, some swaying to the music that is thundering out from the house, others smooching in corners where they don't think they can be seen.

'It's OK, you don't have to stay,' I tell Hugo. 'I'll be fine.'

'Sure you will,' he agrees, yawning and stretching his arms above his head, 'but to be honest, I prefer it out here. I'm not really a party person.'

'So what kind of person are you?' I hear myself ask. Honestly, rum and coke has a lot to answer for.

'Bossy, demanding, inquisitive, or downright crazy, depending on who you ask!' he replies cheerfully. 'Which version would you like me to be?'

I can't help smiling.

'How about crazy?' I tease, swigging some more water. 'The others sound too much like all the other people in my life.'

'OK, crazy it is!' He jumps to his feet. 'Come on!'

He grabs my hand and looks wildly round the garden. 'Up here!'

Within a second he is scaling the garden wall, his feet squashing bits of ivy as he climbs.

'Come on!' He leans down and offers me a hand.

'I can't – I mean, we . . .'

'Hugo! What are you doing?'

Anya, Viki and a couple of guys from Year Thirteen are gawping up at him.

'Emily wanted to do something crazy!' he shouts. 'But now she's chickening out!'

This, I feel, is a slight stretching of the truth.

'I'll come!' Within a flash, Anya is kicking off her kitten heels. 'Give me a leg up, Tim!'

'Go on, Em!' Viki urges under her breath. 'Don't let that little tart steal your guy!'

'He's not my guy!' I hiss under my breath.

'Well, he'd like to be,' she retorts. 'Trust me – I know the signs.'

I'm not sure how or why I find myself on top of the wall, barefooted and dancing to the sounds of Echo Chamber's latest hit. I'm not even sure how all the other people managed to get up here as well; all I know is that there are about a dozen of us, clapping and stamping and laughing.

'Crazy enough?' Hugo asks and grabs me round the waist.

'Just about!' I giggle as Viki flashes her camera yet again and almost falls of the wall.

'Well, at least that's one wish come true!'

He laughs at my puzzled frown. 'When I asked you this afternoon whether there was anything in your life, other than tennis, you said "I wish!"' he reminds me. 'Now you can add wall dancing to your list!'

Suddenly I feel like a balloon that someone has just pierced with a pin. For a couple of hours, I'd forgotten all about Felix and leaving Trinity High and spending the next umpteen years slogging my guts out on a tennis court. Now it's all come flooding back.

'What did I say?' Hugo has stopped dancing and is staring into my eyes. 'You're crying!'

'I am not!'

He raises a finger to my cheek and I can feel wetness.

'It's just the cold air!' I snap, horrified to discover that he's right. I guess it's the drink – it always makes me go soppy.

'Come on!' he orders, then drops into a sitting position and slides down off the wall. 'Jump!'

He opens his arms wide and beckons me. It looks an awful long way down.

'I can't . . .'

'Course you can!' He laughs. 'I'm here to catch you!'

'Ah, isn't it sweet?' someone murmurs sarcastically in my left ear.

'Hang on!' shouts Viki from the other end of the wall. '*This* I have to catch on film!'

She slithers off the wall and collapses into a small bush.

'Wait!' she yells.

Too right I'll wait. I have absolutely no intention of . . .

'OK, jump!' Viki has the viewfinder to her eye. 'Now!'

They're all looking, stamping, egging me on.

I take a deep breath and hurl myself off the wall, straight into Hugo's arms. He smells of pine and sea spray and his hands press into my back. He doesn't seem in any hurry to let go.

Everyone's cheering.

'That's the best shot ever!' declares Viki. 'Look!'

There in the little screen on the camera is me, flying through the air with Hugo's arms outstretched in a V to catch me.

'That,' breathes Hugo, 'is one hell of a picture!'

It is too. It occurs to me that it's the first picture of me that I've seen in ages without a tennis racquet in my hand and a fixed grin on my face. I like it a lot.

Everyone starts drifting off but Hugo is rooted to the spot.

'So?' he inquires, his hands still around my waist. 'Are you going to train with Felix Fordyce or not?'

'I guess I don't have any . . . how did you know about Felix?' I gasp.

'I'm a reporter,' he says. 'It's my business to find things out. Your mum said you had to go and see Felix, all the cuttings I had read about you mentioned the fact that you were in the running for a tennis scholarship . . . it didn't take a genius to put two and two together.'

He runs his fingers through his hair.

'You don't want to do it, do you?'

'Of course I do,' I hear myself reply. 'It's a brilliant opportunity – most people would give their right arm to be in my shoes.'

'Which wouldn't help their game much, would it?'

I can't help laughing.

'OK, so we agree it's a great chance, we agree that loads of players would be over the moon – but you're not, right?'

'No.'

I shouldn't have said that. Why did I say that?

'If you print that, I'll deny I ever said it, I'll . . .' An image of Felix laying down the law swims before my eyes.

Hugo holds his hand in the air and takes two steps backwards in mock terror. 'I won't, I won't!' he protests. 'So what *do* you want to do with your life?'

I shiver. I'm not sure whether it's because the evening is getting cool or whether it's because I know what reaction I'll get if I tell him.

'Emmy! Mum's here!' Charlie is waving at me frantically from the French doors.

'Got to go,' I say.

'Wait!' He grabs my wrist. 'Can I see you again? Tomorrow?'

I'm gobsmacked. He must be nineteen, and he's dishy and he wants to see me?

'Why?'

He laughs. 'Why? Because I like you and . . .'

He stops.

'And?'

'And I think we have a lot in common,' he adds, averting his eyes and colouring up slightly.

'Oh, sure!'

I think the hangover is kicking in. I feel jangly and edgy and just want to get to bed.

'You want to see me so that you write about me in the paper!' I snap. 'Well, forget it!'

Hugo doesn't reply. He stares at me and then turns away and walks back into the house.

'Emily, Mum's going ballistic!' Charlie comes running towards me. 'We have to get going!'

While we're getting our coats and saying our goodbyes, my eyes dart all over the place looking for Hugo. I shouldn't have snapped the way I did; I just want to say I'm sorry. But I can't see him anywhere.

'Good party?' Charlie's mum asks as we climb into the car.

'Great,' raves Charlie. 'Emily pulled!'

'Pulled what?' asks Mrs Henderson anxiously. 'Are you all right, dear?'

No, I want to scream above Charlie's hysterical giggles. I've messed up again.

'Fine, thanks!' I say. Maybe it's just as well I probably

won't have the chance to follow my dream. Liars would hardly be welcome in the job I want to do.

I might as well stick at tennis and be done with it.

❧

'So go on, tell me!' Charlie pulls the duvet up round her neck and grins at me.

'Tell you what?' I yawn. I can guess what she's on about, but I'm tired and fed up with myself and all I want to do is sleep.

'Hugo, of course!' she urges. 'What happened?'

'Nothing happened,' I retort, and then decide to come clean. 'Except that I messed up big time.'

By the time I tell her what I said to Hugo, she's looking at me as if I have a screw loose.

'I don't get it,' she says. 'One of the fittest guys at the party takes a real interest in you and you bite his head off. You don't know how lucky you are . . .'

'You keep saying that!' I interrupt.

'So maybe it's true!' she counters. 'Anyway, what's with all the secrecy? If you don't want to do this tennis thing, what does it matter *who* knows?'

'I haven't told my mother yet and –'

'So tell her!' Charlie sounds impatient. 'Honestly, Emily, I'm sorry but you are making such a big thing of this! So you want to stay on and do A Levels and go to uni? What's the big deal? It's hardly unconventional, is it?'

I count to ten in my head, and then explain to her about

all the money Mum has pumped into my coaching and how she and Lally expect me to make the sport my career.

'But it's not up to them, is it?' she reasons. 'They've had their lives – they can't expect to live yours for you.' She yawns. 'Anyway, you can always take up the tennis again after university,' she says.

'It doesn't work like that – and anyway, I don't want to,' I tell her.

'So what do you want to do – with your life, I mean?' she asks, snuggling down and switching off the bedside light.

Whether it's because it's dark, or because I simply have to test the waters with someone and Charlie's my best friend, I don't know, but before I really have time to think about it, I've told her.

She doesn't say a word. I knew it; she thinks I'm totally weird. She's either going to laugh out loud, or tell me I'm crazy or worse – go and tell everyone else I'm crazy.

'Emily,' she breathes.

Here we go.

'That's amazing,' she whispers.

What? 'You mean, you're not going to tell me I'm stupid?'

'The only thing that's stupid is that you haven't told your mum. You have to tell her, Emily. She'll be so proud of you!'

I shake my head and then realise she can't see me in the dark. 'I don't think so,' I sigh. 'I think she'll throw a total wobbly.'

'Don't be silly!' retorts Charlie. 'I mean, what you want

to do is so much more – oh, I don't know, worthwhile, I guess – than playing a load of tennis!'

'Try telling my mother that,' I mutter.

'If you don't get a move on, I will do just that!' she declares. 'I'll march over to your place and I'll –'

'Don't you dare!'

'Well, you know what you have to do then, don't you? Night night!'

She's right. I have to tell her.

Whenever I think about the future, I know that these plans are the only ones that make me feel warm inside. The rest leave me cold. And that must mean something, mustn't it?

'Mum, there's something you should know. I'm not going to tennis academy, I'm doing A Levels, going to uni and then . . .'

No. I can't put it like that.

'Mum, how would it be if we just carried on like before? I stay on at school, play in a few matches . . .'

No. That's ridiculous. Four A Levels and tennis tournaments don't mix.

'Mum, this is my life and I have to lead it my way.'

That's Charlie's version. She's got this book called *Tell It Like It Is – Assertiveness for Teens* and she reads chunks of it to me over breakfast.

'Your problem,' she informs me, 'is that you want to

keep everyone happy all the time and the only person who ends up miserable is you. And that is just stupid.'

'You don't understand,' I tell her. 'After my dad ran off to Argentina with that woman, Mum was in pieces. She put all her energies into me and my tennis and –'

'EMILY!' Charlie almost spits her Rice Krispies in my face. 'So your mum got divorced? OK, that's sad – but it doesn't give her the right to tell you what to do and it certainly shouldn't make you do things just because you feel sorry for her!'

She slams the book shut and thrusts it into my hands.

'Go on, take it,' she says. 'You need all the help you can get.'

I don't argue. With Charlie, you just don't.

'Which reminds me – are you coming with me?' I asked.

'To church?' Charlie glances at her watch. 'Course I am. Perhaps God'll have more luck sorting you out than I do!'

I guess that's another reason why Charlie is my best friend. She doesn't laugh at me for going to church. In fact, she quite likes coming with me, although I think that has a lot to do with Adam Foster who sings in the choir and keeps winking at her during the sermon. And she doesn't talk about God in hushed whispers; she chats to him like I do – only her chats are mainly about boys and freckles and mine are about the future. I wouldn't admit any of this to anyone else, mind you. These days, I keep quiet about church. I know you're supposed to spread the word, but Trinity High isn't the place to do it, not with people like

Verity Grant and Freya Pearson making snide comments all the time.

We get there early because Charlie likes to sit where she can see Adam in the choir stalls. Charlie spends most of the service digging me in the ribs and saying things like, 'See, it's a sign!' and 'Told you so!' At first, I thought she was ecstatic because Adam stared straight at her while he sang the solo verse of 'All Things Bright and Beautiful', but as she goes on prodding me at five-minute intervals I realise it's because the vicar keeps going on about doing what we know is right even when the entire world seems against us. He makes it sound so simple, but then, he doesn't live with my mother. Actually, I think he's a bit naïve; he says all you have to do is pray and you'll be given the strength to do anything. I prayed for strength to lose my last match and what happened?

I did give it a go again this morning, though. I prayed really hard, the sort of screwed-up-eyes praying where you hold your breath and try desperately not to start thinking about Rufus's thigh muscles or whether you'll get an A for your Biology essay. I prayed that I'd find the right way to explain to Mum about going to university and about what I want to do after that. I kept hoping the words would leap into my brain but they didn't. The only things that are leaping now are the butterflies in my stomach.

It's not that I'm scared of Mum; it's just that I know how much she wants me to be famous and earn wads of money. Money means a lot to my mother. Dad used to send money but now it's down to a small cheque on my birthday.

Which is why I don't want to make Mum any more upset or cross than she is already. I'm all she's got left, as she keeps telling me. She also keeps telling me that I have a God-given talent – which is quite funny when you consider that she doesn't believe in God and can't work out why I like going to St Luke's so much.

'You won't have to be stuck in some boring job,' she keeps telling me. 'You'll travel the world, you'll be someone!'

Well, if I ever get to do what I really want I'm going to travel the world – but somehow I don't think it's quite the way Mum has in mind.

'Just get over to your grandmother's house and tell it like it is!' Charlie instructs me as we walk out of church. 'Your gran will stick up for you – that's what grandparents do.'

She has a point. Lally and I have always got on really well; she's more of a mate than a relation. In fact, if I get a move on, I might just get there before Mum arrives and have the chance to talk to Lally on my own, smooth the ground a bit and . . .

Sugar. My mobile's ringing. It's sure to be Mum wondering where I am.

'Emily – is that you?' It's not Mum. It's a very sexy male voice.

I don't know any sexy males. 'Yes?'

'It's Hugo.'

Oh no. Oh good . . . What do I say?

'Oh hi!' How's that for a witty reply? 'How did you get my number?'

My conversational ability amazes me sometimes.

'Rufus,' he says.

Rufus has my mobile number? Rufus cares enough to . . .

'Well, his sister actually – Viki, isn't it?' Another dream bites the dust.

'Look, I need to see you,' he goes on. 'There's something really important I want to ask you.' His voice is having the most extraordinary effect on my heart rate.

'Well, I . . .'

'It won't take long,' he insists. 'Please.'

I don't have many guys pleading for my attention – not unless you count the ones who see mixed doubles as an excuse to pat your bottom on the tennis court.

'OK then,' I tell him, trying not to sound too enthusiastic. 'But it can't be till later – I have to have lunch with my grandmother. How about this evening?'

'Too late – I mean, I'd rather you made it earlier if you could.'

Come to think of it, I might need an escape route after confronting my mother.

'Four-thirty, then,' I propose.

'Great!' He sounds as if I've just bailed him out of jail. 'Where?'

'It'll have to be somewhere near my grandmother's house,' I tell him. 'What about the Seagull Café, just past the West Pier,' I suggest.

'Brilliant! See you then! Have a good lunch!'

I wish.

'Emily! At last! Where have you been?' Mum flings open Lally's front door as the gate slams behind me. So much for a quiet chat with my grandmother.

'Church,' I reply. 'I told you. The service ran on a bit . . .'

That's another lie, but I can hardly tell her that I had to go round the block three times to rehearse what I'm about to say.

'Lally's got a surprise,' she whispers. 'It's champagne – but don't let on I told you!' She pushes me into the sitting room just as my grandmother emerges from the kitchen, wearing an enormous Stars and Stripes apron and brandishing a bottle.

'Darling!' Lally sweeps me into a breath-crushing hug. 'What do you say to a glass of champers?'

'Champagne?' I try to sound astonished and my mother gives me a wink of approval. 'What's this for?'

'It's obvious, darling,' Mum interjects as Lally starts prising off the cork holding the bottle at arm's length. 'Your triumph yesterday! Right, Ma?'

'Well, yes, of course.' Lally bites her lip. 'That and also . . .'

'You found your bracelet!' Mum cries. 'Is that it?'

Lally's face falls. 'Sadly, no,' she sighs. She gives the cork a final twist and it bursts from the bottle with a very satisfying pop.

'But,' she says, grabbing a glass as the bubbly froths over her hand, 'I thought we could drink to the future!' She passes us both a glass and pours one for herself.

'What a lovely idea!' Mum raises her glass. 'To the future! To Emily and the Grand Slam!'

Say it. Say it now. You have to. You can't keep this charade going forever.

'Mum . . .' I begin, and then realise that although my mouth is moving, no sound is coming out.

'To *all* our futures!' Lally says firmly. 'Emmy's, yours and mine!' She takes a huge gulp of champagne.

'Of course!' Mum is beaming. 'To us – all together under one roof!'

'Mum . . .' This time the word is audible. 'There's something I have to tell you . . .' I turn to Lally '. . . both of you.'

'Really, darling? How intriguing! Let me just bring the lunch through and I'm all ears!' Lally heads for the kitchen.

'What is it?' Mum begins but no way am I going to put my life on the line till Lally gets back.

'I'll just go and help with the dishes,' I mutter hastily, knowing that after sixteen years of nagging me to be more helpful around the house, she wouldn't dare stop me now. I dash to the kitchen and as I push open the swing door, I hear Lally talking to herself.

'Lally . . .'

She jumps out of her skin and almost drops the roasting tin.

'Can I help?'

She looks flushed and flustered. 'Oh – er, yes, thank you darling!' She flicks a finger across her cheek and I realise that her eyes are damp.

'Shall I go upstairs after lunch and have a hunt for your bracelet?' I ask her, wrapping my arms round her waist.

She smiles and pats my arm. 'I've looked a dozen times,'

she sighs. 'But it's sweet of you to ask. Now, let's go and hit this Yorkshire pudding before it collapses!'

I don't need to be asked twice. You don't get proper food in my house – not with a mother who believes that all future tennis stars need fat-free, calorie-reduced, totally organic everything.

'Are there parsnips?' I ask.

Lally grins. 'And two sorts of potato!'

I think I'll wait to drop my bombshell until pudding time. I argue better on a full stomach.

'So,' says Mum, putting down her knife and fork and leaning back in her chair, 'tomorrow we must go to see your head teacher and tell him you'll be leaving at the end of term!'

'No!' This outburst surprises even me.

Mum turns to me, astounded. 'What do you mean, no?' she demands. 'It's only polite to let him know at once – there's a waiting list for the Sixth Form and someone else can take your place and . . .'

'No, they can't!'

Lally is watching me but not saying a word.

'The thing is, Mum,' I begin, taking a deep breath and twisting my napkin in my fingers, 'I don't want to go to the tennis academy.'

For a moment, you could hear a pin drop. But only for a moment.

'You don't want . . . I've never heard anything so ridiculous in my life!'

'It's not ridiculous, it's –'

'Emily, are you mad? You have been working for this ever since you were eight and . . .'

'No, Mum – you have!' No, that came out all wrong. 'I mean, yes, I used to want to make tennis my life but that's changed. I don't want it any more.'

'Oh, *terrific*!' Mum pushes back her chair and jumps to her feet. 'The top coach in British tennis offers you a scholarship and *you* don't want it! And what, may I ask, *do* you want?'

Careful. Don't say it all in one go.

'I'd like to stay on at school, do A Levels and go to university,' I blurt out.

I can see that Mum is trying to remain calm. 'Look, Em,' she says, putting a hand on my shoulder, 'I know the thought of leaving all your friends must be a bit daunting, but just think! This is the beginning of a whole career – it's your chance to *be* someone, to make a name for yourself and –'

'That's just the point!' I know I shouldn't shout, but I can't help it. 'That's what it's all about, isn't it? Making a name for myself, being famous, winning prizes! It's all me, me, me!'

'And what's wrong with that?' Mum demands. 'In this world, my girl, if you don't look out for number one, no one else will!'

'And what about everybody else?' I demand, struggling not to cry. 'What if everyone thought like you do – what then?'

'Oh, so the way I think is wrong now, is it?' Mum thumps her fist on the table and the cutlery rattles. 'Don't you realise what I have sacrificed in order to give you the very best start in life . . .'

'I didn't ask you to, did I?' The words are out before I can stop them and I see Mum flinch as if I had hit her.

'I'm sorry – I . . . I didn't mean it to sound like that,' I stammer. 'It's been great, honestly Mum. I've enjoyed all the tournaments and being in the county squad and everything. It's just that now . . .'

'Now you want to throw it all away . . .'

'Let Emily finish, Ruth!' Lally has been so silent through all this that I'm almost surprised to see her still sitting at the head of the table, her eyes fixed on my face.

'What is it you really want to do, Emmy?' Lally continues. 'A Levels, you said?'

I nod. 'Economics, English, French and General Studies,' I gabble. 'I've talked to my year tutor and –'

'But not, it seems, to your mother!' Mum interjects. 'Or your coach! Wasting your teacher's time over . . .'

Lally waves a hand to silence her, and to my amazement Mum stops in mid-sentence.

'And university?' Lally urges.

'There's not going to be any university,' my mother mutters under her breath. Both Lally and I pretend we haven't heard.

'I want to . . .' The words are sticking in my throat. It's not because I'm changing my mind; it's because I don't think I could bear it if they both laugh.

'Yes?' Lally lays her hand on mine and smiles encouragingly.

'I want to work for an international aid agency,' I blurt out. 'UNICEF or Compassion UK or someone like that. In Rwanda or Macedonia or . . .'

'Are you raving mad?'

My mother is staring at me as though I have suggested taking up refuse collection as a career.

'I don't think she's mad at all.' Lally's voice is soft but its firmness stops my mother in her tracks.

'I think that's a wonderful ambition,' she says, turning to me. 'So what will you have to study at uni? Sociology? Economics?'

I shrug. 'Probably. Possibly. The thing is, I don't really know . . .'

'You see?' My mother is in there like a ton of bricks. 'She hasn't thought it through at all! She's just acting on some fleeting whim . . .'

'No, I'm not! The reason I don't know is because I kept hoping that I *would* change my mind. I didn't bother finding out about courses, A Levels, all that stuff, because I knew how much my tennis meant to you.'

'I thought it did to you . . .' My mother's voice has taken on a pleading note, but I'm not stopping now.

'It did, but not now. I don't *want* to let you down, Mum; I'm not doing this out of spite. I'm doing it because in my heart I know it's right for me . . .'

'Then,' interjects Lally, 'you must do it. Follow your dream – that's all that really matters.'

'Oh my God!' My mother's face has turned bright red. 'That's rich, coming from you! That wasn't what you thought forty years ago, was it?'

I haven't a clue what she's on about but Lally doesn't seem fazed.

'No, you're right!' she admits. 'I didn't think it sixty years ago, either.'

'What?' Now Mum looks as bewildered as I feel.

'Since we're on the subject of the future,' Lally says, dabbing her mouth with her napkin, 'it's probably time I told you . . . what's that smell?' She sniffs loudly. 'Oh no! My apple pie!' With that, she jumps up and rushes out of the room.

For a moment, neither Mum nor I speak. Then Mum reaches out a hand and touches my arm.

'Look, love,' she begins, quite clearly trying to be calm and responsive, 'you have to be sensible about this. You have a real talent, a gift for tennis. With hard work and the best coaching, you could really make the big time.'

'But . . .'

'No, let *me* finish!' she says, throwing Lally's words back at me. 'By the time you're thirty, you could have earned enough money to retire – you could become a tennis commentator, you could even go to university then, loads of people do and –'

'Mum, that's NOT what I want!'

'OK, so then – after you've made enough money to be secure for life, you could do your charity work!' Her nose actually wrinkles as she says the word *charity*.

I try a different approach. 'I'm not saying I won't play any tennis,' I explain. 'I love it as a game and it will always be a hobby. But I *won't* make it my career.'

'But aid agencies!' Mum protests. 'You can't go and work in the back of beyond – haven't you seen the TV pictures? No sanitation, awful diseases, land mines . . . it's hardly the place one chooses to live and work.'

'Some people don't have the choice,' I tell her.

'Oh for God's sake, Emily! Stop being so bloody pious! I suppose that church is responsible for all this? You really are . . .'

'Here we are!' Lally strides back into the room, holding a rather overdone apple pie in one hand and a jug of custard in the other. 'Bit burnt round the edges but charcoal is good for grouchiness!'

She throws my mother one of her fierce glances.

'Can't you make your granddaughter see sense?' demands Mum, as Lally plunges a knife into the pie. 'She's determined to throw her life away on . . .'

This has gone on long enough. 'So what was it you were going to tell us, Lally?' I ask brightly. 'You were about to say something when the pie burned.'

'Yes,' says Lally, passing plates across the table and sitting down. 'No time like the present.'

She takes a deep breath, picks up her spoon and puts it down again.

'I am going to live in America.'

'You are *what*?' my mother gasps.

'America?' I can't believe it – I mean, I know she adores

the place, but she's old, for heaven's sake. Old people don't just up and go halfway round the world to live. Besides, she's my grandmother. I love her. She can't.

'Wolf Creek, Montana, to be precise,' she continues, avoiding our gaze. 'It's a beautiful place, wide river, stunning mountains . . .'

'Never mind the guided tour!' explodes my mother. 'Ma, have you taken leave of your senses?'

'I have never been more sensible in my life,' stresses Lally.

'But you don't know anyone in America!' I say. 'You'll be lonely and . . .'

'I do know someone in America,' she says. 'That's why I'm going.'

She pauses and takes a deep breath.

'Darlings, I do so want you to be happy for me,' she pleads. 'You see, I'm going to Montana to get married.'

I'll say one thing for Lally; she certainly knows how to take the heat off of me. My mother is in the sitting room in floods of tears, Lally is slamming crockery into the dishwasher like a woman possessed and I'm making tea. We always make tea in a crisis in our family. Something tells me we'll be drinking quite a lot of it over the next few hours.

After Lally made her dramatic announcement, my mother went ballistic. It made her reaction to my plans seem like a minor blip; this time it was major histrionics. I can't really blame her – I mean, my grandmother is almost seventy-five years old so she can't be marrying for love or sex or anything. And she can't *really* want to leave Mum and me. Old people are supposed to want to be with their families. For once, I'm on my mum's side.

'So who is this man?' my mother demanded. 'Some money-grabbing Yank on the make, is he?' Tact is not my mother's strongest attribute.

'He is a very dear man, whom I've known for a long time.'

'Oh yes? How long?' my mother retorted.

'Since my sixteenth birthday,' Lally replied. 'Since I was Emily's age.' She smiles at me. 'I've known him – no, let's be honest – I've *loved* him for almost sixty years.'

My mother went so pale that for a moment I thought she was either going to throw up or pass out.

'But you got married – to Dad!'

Lally nodded. 'I know,' she sighed. 'I thought I was doing the sensible thing . . .' She turned to me. 'Emily, you must go where your heart leads you. If you don't, you could spend a lifetime regretting it.'

'Oh – so you regret Dad, do you?' my mother exploded. 'And I suppose you regret having me as well? Is that it?'

'Darling, of course not!' Lally cried. 'Having you was the one thing that kept me going – you were my everything!' She ran a hand across her eyes. 'I was so proud of you,' she went on. 'You were clever, spunky . . . In fact,' she added with a faint smile, 'I felt that you were a miniature version of me.'

'I seem to recall,' my mother said, her voice cold, 'that my spunkiness, as you call it, was the one thing you did your utmost to quash!'

Lally bit her lip. 'You were sixteen, darling. I thought I was doing the best for you.' She sighed. 'It's only now that I realise that I did it all wrong – that's why I want Emily to . . .'

'Just leave Emily out of this!' stormed my mother. 'Emily is my concern. It seems you can't even conduct your own life in a mature fashion so don't try telling my daughter what she can and can't do!' And with that she burst into tears.

For all I know, she's still crying. I don't know what to say or do.

'Lally,' I say tentatively, as my grandmother slams the dishwasher shut and punches the 'ON' button, 'are you sure that going to America is a good idea? I mean, couldn't you just go for lots of holidays and see this guy?'

She smiles at me and shakes her head. 'I've been doing that for years,' she says.

She has?

'It's just not enough,' she goes on. 'Losing that bracelet was the final straw.'

'The bracelet?' What does the bracelet have to do with it? Perhaps she's going senile.

'Emily, darling, I'm not a girl any more. I don't know how long I've got left on this earth – but however short or long it may be, I just want to spend it with Zack.'

Suddenly I find I'm crying. I don't know whether it's

because Mum is so angry with me, or whether it's the thought of Lally going miles away and maybe dying before I get to see her again, but once I've started I can't stop.

Lally comes and puts her arms round me. 'I think,' she says, 'that it's time I told you – and your mother – the truth.'

I look at her through blurred eyes.

'What do you mean?'

'Come with me.' She takes my hand and we walk through to the sitting room. Mum has stopped crying, but she's sitting on the edge of one of the armchairs, twisting her handkerchief round and round in her fingers.

'Ruth, I haven't been completely honest with you,' Lally blurts out. 'But I want to make up for that now. I want to tell you both the whole story – from beginning to end.'

'What story?' My mother blows her nose. 'More non-sense about . . .'

'Mum, don't!' I beg. 'Let Lally speak.'

'I want to tell you how it all began,' says Lally. 'Just sit down and give me half an hour. Please?'

My mother shrugs. 'OK,' she says. 'Go on then. It can't get any worse.'

Lally sits on the battered leather sofa in the corner of the room and gestures to me to sit beside her.

'It all started in 1943,' she says. 'I remember it as though it were yesterday. It was September 21st . . .'

'Your birthday,' I interrupt.

'Yes, my sixteenth birthday,' Lally sighs. 'I wasn't expecting it to be much fun – we were in the middle of the war, everything was rationed, and my father had been killed eleven months before.' She pauses. 'In fact, if it hadn't been for my friend Vi, it would have ended up as a day like any other. But Vi had plans . . .'

ALICE
September 1943

'SO YOU WILL COME, won't you? Ally? ALICE!'

A sharp elbow in my ribs roused me from my day-dreaming.

'Sorry,' I murmured. 'What did you say?'

'Don't you ever listen, Miss Head in the Clouds?' Vi demanded grinning good-naturedly, grabbing my arm as we took a short cut across another bomb site. 'I said that because it's your birthday we ought to do something special and . . .'

'Some birthday!' I muttered, kicking a piece of shrapnel out of my path. 'I know I shouldn't complain, but don't you wish things could go back to the way they were before this horrid war?'

I thought back to that morning when I unwrapped my presents – two hankies and a bar of soap. It wasn't Mum's fault; what with rationing and money being tight, everyone was in the same boat. And I knew that when I got home, Mum would have made me a birthday cake – but it would be one of those awful dried egg sponges that taste like cardboard, and, of course, there wouldn't be any icing.

'Well, the war's here and there isn't much we can do about it, is there?' Vi urged. 'At least we're alive, unlike poor

Dora and Pat and . . .'

She paused and squeezed my hand.

'. . . and my dad,' I finished for her, giving up any attempt to hide what was really making me miserable.

'Sorry,' she whispered.

'It's OK,' I assured her, 'I'm pretty much over it now.'

That was a barefaced lie. I felt as if I'd never get over it – never forget the day the telegram came with those awful words *We regret to inform you*, always hear in my head my mother's ear-piercing wail before she collapsed in a faint on the hall lino.

Vi gave me a quick hug.

'Well, I was talking to Pamela, and we've decided that we are going to cheer you up,' she announced. 'You're coming dancing with us this evening – and don't try getting out of it!'

'Dancing?' I stared at her. I couldn't go dancing – not with Dad shot out of the skies in a thousand pieces.

'Yes, Alice,' she said patiently. 'People do, you know. You're sixteen – you can't go on sitting at home with your nose in a book every night!'

'But . . .' I began, frantically trying to think of an excuse not to go. It might have been eleven months since Dad got killed but somehow dancing . . .

Vi squeezed my hand again. 'Do you think your dad would want you to miss out on life?' she asked gently. 'It would break his heart.'

I nodded slowly. People kept saying that kind of thing to me, and deep down, I knew they were right. Life, as everyone on the radio kept telling us, had to go on.

'Besides,' Vi declared. 'Now you are sixteen, I, as your dearest friend and an older woman . . .'

'By nine months!' I protested.

'. . . I have decided to launch you into society!'

I burst out laughing. You couldn't stay miserable for long in Vi's company; she was one of those daft people who saw the funny side of everything – even war.

She grinned. 'That's better! So you'll come?'

I nodded. After all, I didn't have to dance; I could just sit and watch.

'I'll call for you at seven sharp,' she said. 'Must dash – my shift started ten minutes ago. Have fun!'

I sighed. She made it sound as if I was off on a picnic. It was all right for Vi; she had never wanted to stay on at school and was only too happy working in the canteen at the local munitions factory. But thanks to Adolf Hitler, my life was in ruins – how could I become a history teacher if I was stuck in a grocer's shop all day? Teaching was all I had ever wanted to do since I was about eight years old and Miss Bayliss had told me a dozen times that if I worked really hard I could get to teacher training college.

'The world is your oyster, Alice,' she used to say.

Some oyster. After Dad was killed, Mum decided I had to leave school and pay my way. I tried to argue, but there was no point.

'Your father died for his country, Alice Jupp,' she said. 'The least you can do is work for it.'

After that, what could I say?

'Don't worry, Alice,' Miss Bayliss had reassured me when she found me in floods of tears in the toilets the day after my fifteenth birthday, 'you can go to college after the war – there's still plenty of time.'

The glimmer of hope that comment raised didn't last long.

'High-falutin nonsense!' my mother had snorted when I repeated the conversation to her. 'Stanley's not going to want a wife with ideas above her station and . . .'

'What Stanley does or doesn't want is hardly the point, since I'm not remotely interested in him!' I snapped back at her as I had a dozen times before.

'You could do a lot worse!' my mother retorted. 'They've got prospects, the Turnbull family – there's that nice little drapery business and I hear that the grandmother isn't short of a bob or two. And besides, Stanley's a bright lad – he could go far.'

'So could I, Mum!'

'You're a girl,' she replied. She was one for stating the obvious, my mother. 'Your father always said that he didn't like the idea of a girl working because . . .'

I wanted to shout at her, but I couldn't. I knew how desperately she missed Dad – she'd hung on his every word while he was alive and now she was forever telling me what he would or would not have wanted. It was as if by doing what Dad would have done, she felt closer to him.

But I still had one half-hearted try at making her see things differently.

'But Mum, you say you enjoy working at the Underground station . . .'

'That's different,' she began. 'That's because there's a war on and . . .'

I didn't really listen to the reply because I knew it would be more of the same. There's a war on; we're fighting back; things will get back to normal in peacetime.

By that, of course, she meant that I could marry Stanley, settle down (oh, how I hated those words!) and have a family. I couldn't believe how she and Stanley's mother conspired to push us together. They'd been doing it since we were about thirteen. It wasn't that I had anything against marriage, but I wasn't like a lot of my friends, whose lives revolved around finding a chap who was willing to slip a ring on their finger. I wanted to travel to all the places I had read about in my history books – to the battle sites of Culloden and Bannockburn in Scotland, to Warwick Castle and Fotheringhay and Hadrian's Wall – perhaps one day even to America to see where the Pilgrim Fathers landed. Marriage – to Stanley or anyone else – just wasn't for me.

Still, I thought, as I hung my cardigan on the hook in the back room of the shop and slipped into the revolting green overall that was two sizes too big for me, at least Stanley wasn't around at the moment to linger, all gooey-eyed and pathetic, outside Greg's Grocery every evening. Two days after his eighteenth birthday, he'd joined up and gone to France to fight alongside his brother, Alf. I was fond of both of them, in a sort of sisterly way. We'd played together as kids and they had always looked out for me when the bullies from Tarrant Street tried to grab my skipping rope or tease me by putting spiders down my jumper. Once Alf had gone off to war, Stanley had started to get all romantic and, frankly, I wasn't interested. His mum kept dropping hints about how happy she would be to see us together once the war was over. She had married at nineteen and mine at eighteen and somehow they both seemed to think that I would do the same. I didn't tell her that once the war was over I would have better things to do that tie myself to any man.

Vi said there was something seriously wrong with me and that if Stanley took a fancy to her, she'd leap at the chance.

'Have him!' I told her. 'You're welcome!'

She did her best, flirting with him, telling him how handsome he was but it didn't work. Stanley didn't want Vi – he wanted me.

'Alice, I hate to bother you, but I've got a shop to run here!' Mrs Smart slammed a box of tinned fruit in front of me, bringing me back sharply from my thoughts. 'Stack these in the window and price 'em – if you can spare the time!'

I thought over and over again that day, as I stamped people's ration books, or told them yet another way to make an ounce of bacon and a tired cauliflower into a nourishing meal for five, that nothing exciting was ever going to happen to me again. It was my sixteenth birthday and I was going to spend it in the dullest job on earth while real life passed me by.

Even the thought of dancing at the Palais that evening didn't raise my spirits. I would have much preferred to curl up with the *Life of Queen Victoria,* a book I'd borrowed from the library . . . and besides, it wasn't as if anyone remotely interesting would be there – just boys too young to go and fight and couples making the most of a 24-hour leave.

If I'd known what was actually going to happen, I might have taken a little more time to get ready.

'And I suppose you're going with that Violet?' my mother muttered. 'And she's no better than she ought to be.'

'Mum . . .'

'I don't like it, Alice,' she sighed. 'I've got to work down at the station tonight and I'd rather know you were safe indoors.'

Mum worked as a ticket collector on the Underground, the job my uncle Reggie had before he joined up.

'But Mum,' I protested, 'I'll be just as safe round the corner at the Palais – if a bomb's going to hit me . . .'

'DON'T SAY THAT!' she shouted.

'It's my birthday, Mum,' I pleaded, changing tack. 'And you did say we mustn't let Hitler think he's got us down.' Actually, it was Dad who had said that in all his letters home but I knew it would work.

'All right,' she said, breaking into a smile and ruffling my hair the way she used to when I was little. 'Since it's your birthday – but if the air-raid sirens go off, you go to the shelter, do you hear me? None of this being brave nonsense!'

She pulled me towards her and gave me a hug.

'If anything should happen to you . . .'

'It won't, Mum, I promise!' I assured her. 'It's only round the corner and, besides, we won't be late – Vi's mum is working tonight so Vi has to get home by half-past ten to babysit the twins.'

Mum's shoulders dropped in relief.

'That's all right, then,' she said. 'And no ripping off those armbands from your coat, mind. I want you visible in the blackout, you hear me?'

I nodded obediently. Ever since my friend Dora got killed by a bus crashing into her in the blackout, I had stopped worrying about fashion and concentrated on staying alive.

Mum grinned at me.

'And now – guess what I got you for your birthday tea?'

Dried egg sponge, I thought, with a sinking heart, and prepared myself to look ecstatic over a candle stuck in tasteless mess.

Mum pulled open the oven door.

'Ta-da!' she cried, pulling out a baking tray.

'Sausages!' I cried. 'How on earth . . . I mean, you said you didn't have enough coupons?' Ever since rationing started, mealtimes had become deadly boring.

Mum chuckled. 'I let old Frank down at the butcher's hold my hand over the counter three times last week,' she winked. 'My reward was three sausages – two for you, as you're the birthday girl, and one for me.'

My mouth was watering so much that I didn't bother telling my mother that she was far too old to be flirting with strange men across a meat counter.

'Your dad loved a sausage,' she sighed, prodding them with a fork and dumping them on to plates. 'I remember one day . . .'

I couldn't bear to hear Mum talking about what Dad used to do; I'd promised myself that I would be strong for her, and I knew that if she started on one of her stories, I'd only cry and that would spoil everything.

'Can I have a bath before I go out?' I asked. Silly really, but it was the first thing that came into my head.

'A bath?' She stared at me as if I'd suggested dancing naked in the street. 'And waste even more soap and water? Don't you know there's a war on?'

As if I could ever forget.

'Alice, why are you wearing socks?' Vi looked at me pityingly and then yanked up her skirt and twirled around in front of me. 'This is what real women are wearing!'

'Stockings!' I gasped, as the queue to get into the Palais shuffled nearer the door. 'How on earth did you get hold of those?'

Vi burst out laughing.

'They're fake, silly!' she giggled. 'It's called Liquid Silk –

you paint the stuff on, draw a line on the back of your leg to look like a seam and hey presto!'

Suddenly I felt ridiculous. I was wearing one of Mum's old skirts that she had altered to fit me and although I had put curlers in for a whole hour before coming out, my mousy hair refused to wave fashionably but instead stuck out like a porcupine's quills. Vi, on the other hand, looked like a million dollars – and she was wearing make-up which my mother banned because she said it was the stuff of the devil.

Very dramatic, my mother.

'Come on!' Vi pulled me forward into the dim light of the dance hall. 'There's Pam over there by . . . hey, who is that gorgeous fellow she's with?'

I followed Vi's gaze. Pam was perched on the corner of a table, swinging her bare legs and gazing up at a tall blond guy in uniform.

'American!' breathed Vi, as the band burst into a foxtrot. 'I just knew it was our lucky night!' She grabbed my arm and dragged me across the dance floor, dodging the smooching couples.

'This is Brad!' Pam clutched the guy's arm possessively and threw a warning look in Vi's direction. You couldn't blame her; Vi was boy mad and I could see that she was eyeing this one up and down greedily.

'I'm Vi!' she simpered. 'Are there any more where you came from?'

'Vi!' I hissed under my breath. I could feel colour sweeping across my face even though Brad hadn't given me so much as a glance.

He laughed. 'Sure are!' he shouted above the noise of the dancers doing the Hokey Cokey. 'Come on – my pals could do with a bit of cheering up!'

He grabbed Pam's hand and gestured to Vi and me to follow him.

'We can't . . .' I muttered to Vi, but she simply gave me a pitying look and carried on regardless.

There were three of them at the table. Two were sitting there, smoking and talking, but the third was standing with his back to them, staring into space.

'Hey guys, I've brought you some entertainment!' Brad cried. 'This is Pam – but hands off her, she's mine – and this is Vi and . . .'

He hesitated and looked at me with a slight frown.

'Alice,' I whispered.

'Alice,' he repeated. 'Meet Chuck and Grant and . . .' He thumped the third guy on the back. 'Hey, Zack! Stop day-dreaming and meet Alice!'

The guy turned around.

And my world went on hold.

He was like one of those film stars I drooled over at the Embassy each week. He had dark curly hair, grey-green eyes and shoulders as broad as a cowboy's.

He stared at me.

And I stared at him.

And I fell in love.

I know it sounds like some third-rate movie, but that's how it happened. It was as if everyone else had vanished from the dance hall and there was just him and me, locked in this breath-stopping gaze.

'Hi Alice!' His voice was deep and he stressed the first syllable of my name, somehow making it sound far more sophisticated than before.

In the days that followed I tried and tried to remember what happened next, but it was a blur. All I know is that we ended up on the dance floor and that's where we stayed all evening. I told him I couldn't dance and then I discovered that with him, I could. Or rather when I did make a mistake and land on his foot, it didn't seem to matter.

We talked non-stop. He told me where he came from, but since the only places in America that I had ever heard of were New York, Hollywood and San Francisco, it didn't mean much at the time. He was a rear gunner with the US Air Force, based somewhere in Essex, and he was on 48-hour leave.

'Two days to forget all about those endless bombing raids, all that killing and . . .' His voice trailed off.

'And you're spending it in Bethnal Green?' I asked him incredulously. 'I thought all you GIs went up west to the posh spots.'

He gave a little smile, and I suddenly noticed the dark lines under his eyes.

'I persuaded them . . .' he jerked his head towards the opposite side of the room where Brad and Chuck were dancing with Pam and Vi, 'to give me a lift down here. I wanted to search out my roots.'

'You come from round here?' I couldn't believe it. He

was the all-American guy, from his constant gum chewing to his broad accent. He seemed as far removed from the East End as Clark Gable.

'Not me,' he admitted. 'My great-grandparents emigrated from London way back and I kinda wanted to see the house they were living in when my grandmother was born.'

'And have you found it?'

He gave a short laugh. 'Oh sure,' he said. 'One goddamn big hole and a pile of rubble.'

'I'm sorry,' I said and before I realised what I was doing, I squeezed his hand.

He looked down at me, tilting my chin upwards with his finger and gazing into my eyes.

'You are one sweet kid,' he said. 'How old are you?'

That was when I told the first lie – the first of many. 'Eighteen,' I said brightly.

'Really?' He seemed pleased. 'I'm nineteen.'

'You look older,' I said.

'That's what war does,' he sighed, and all the laughter disappeared from his face.

I felt a fool. It was obvious that he wanted to spend his leave forgetting, not being reminded by me.

'And you,' he said, regaining his composure, 'look younger!'

'It's the rationing,' I gabbled on. 'You try four years of being half starved – I guess I'm going, end up stunted for life!'

He threw back his head and roared with laughter.

'Well, I guess we'd better remedy that!' he said, pulling

something from the pocket of his uniform. 'Will this keep the wolf away from the door for a while?'

I stared at his open palm.

'Chocolate!' I breathed. 'Real chocolate!'

'Go on, eat it!' He was grinning. I ripped the paper from the Hershey bar and took a bite. I can taste it now, sweet and smooth and gliding over my tongue. It was so wonderful I wanted it to last forever. I carefully folded the paper over the rest of the bar and slipped it into the pocket of my skirt.

'Don't you like it?' Zack asked, slipping his hand into mine.

'I love it,' I sighed. 'I'm saving it to have in little bits.'

'You're sweet!' he said again. 'Drink?'

As we approached the bar, I saw Vi hopping from one leg to the other and beckoning to me with a lot of head jerking and eye winking.

'Excuse me a minute,' I said to Zack, even though I didn't want to leave his side for one second. 'I'll be back.'

Vi grabbed my hand. 'You have got yourself one handsome . . . !' she began, dragging me towards the Ladies.

'Listen,' I told her sternly, cutting in before she could finish speaking, 'I'm eighteen, OK? Get that? If you tell him I'm only sixteen, I will never, ever, speak to you again as long as I live. And you can tell Pam that goes for her too!'

Vi raised her hands in mock horror.

'Could it be that sweet and innocent little Alice Jupp has finally discovered men?' She giggled, disappearing into one of the cubicles. 'So miracles do still happen!'

'Promise me you won't say anything,' I urged her, raising my voice so she could hear me through the partition.

'Course I won't,' she promised. 'In fact . . .' The flushing of the toilet drowned her words.

'What did you say?'

'Never mind!' she called. 'Just wait and see.'

'*Happy birthday to you, happy birthday to you, happy birthday dear Alice, happy birthday to you!*'

My cheeks were burning. I stared at my feet and vowed to find some way to pay Vi and Pam back for their trickery. Everyone on the dance floor was looking at me – me in my white socks and revolting skirt. What was worse, the lights had been switched on and I could see Zack gazing around the room, obviously eyeing up all the other girls with their sophisticated hairdos and nylon stockings.

'You didn't tell me it was your eighteenth birthday *today*!' he said, as the lights dimmed again and the band struck up 'Don't Fence Me In'. 'You deserve more than a Hershey bar!'

'I'll kill Vi!' I muttered.

'Why?' he asked gently. 'I'm glad she did it.' He shrugged his shoulder. 'Call me vain,' he said, 'but I found it kinda neat to have all those guys looking at me, standing beside the cutest girl in the room.'

He raised his hand and touched my cheek and in that moment, something changed inside me. It was as though a great surge of electricity flooded my whole body, destroying the old Alice Jupp, the slightly dumpy unfashionable East End girl, and transforming her into Alice, the glamorous, witty, sophisticated young woman who could captivate men with one toss of her head.

'Can I see you tomorrow?' Zack leaned closer to me to make himself heard above the beat of the band, snapping me out of my reverie. 'Will you meet me at Victoria Park?'

I couldn't believe it. This gorgeous guy wanted me to go out with him.

'I have to work till five o'clock,' I said eagerly, 'but I could come after that.'

He shook his head. 'Too late – we have to be back at camp by seven,' he said. 'Can't you wangle something? Please?'

I bit my lip. I so much wanted to see him but . . .

'I know I'm being selfish,' he sighed. 'It's just that it's all so awful. Every day, flying over Germany, wondering every second if the next Messerschmitt is going to be one that shoots us down . . .'

He shook his head.

'What I mean is – when something great happens, like meeting you, I don't want it to end.' He gave me a little nudge. 'A bit like you and the Hershey bar!' he laughed.

'I'll come! I'll be at the park at eleven o'clock!'

I didn't know how I was going to do it, but I would find a way. I was feeling things I had never felt before; I wanted to kiss him, yes, but I also wanted to hold him, and reassure him, and take the fear away and never, ever let him out of my sight.

I knew I couldn't do that. But I could spend one more day with him, and no matter what it took, I knew I would do it.

❦

The shop was very busy the next morning. It had been a quiet night – no raids, no bombs, and women were out doing their shopping instead of clearing rubble, boarding up broken windows or comforting friends and neighbours.

I glanced at the clock. Half-past ten. I had to do it now.

'Aaaaah!' I doubled over and clutched my stomach. 'Oh the pain!'

'What is it? What's wrong?' Mrs Smart almost dropped the egg she was wrapping for a customer.

'I feel sick . . . I . . .' And with that, I dashed out through the back room to the outside toilet.

Once there, I counted very slowly to thirty, made a few retching noises just in case anyone had followed me, and then staggered back into the shop.

'I'm so sorry,' I whispered, holding on to the counter. 'I've been horribly sick and . . .'

'Poor lassie!' murmured a woman in the queue. 'She doesn't half look poorly.'

'You send her home, Gladys!' urged another, turning to

Mrs Smart. 'We don't want germs spreading over unwrapped food!' She sniffed, eyeing me as if I was quite probably the transporter of bubonic plague.

'You'd better go,' Mrs Smart said grudgingly, 'although the Lord only knows how I'm going to cope on my own.'

I didn't need to be told twice. I grabbed my coat and, still clutching my stomach for effect, I staggered from the shop. I even managed to walk really slowly to the corner of the street, before breaking into a run and heading straight for Victoria Park.

He was waiting for me where the gate used to be before they pulled it down to turn it into aeroplane parts. He caught me in a big hug, lifted me off the ground and twirled me round and round in his arms. I knew in that moment why people made films and wrote songs about falling in love. This was what being a woman was all about.

'Let's go and eat!' he suggested. 'I saw a café across the way – is that OK?'

Eating out was something I hadn't done in ages and I wasn't about to turn down the offer, even though I knew the menu would just consist of Spam or potato pie.

We ate and we talked.

We walked and we talked.

We sat on park benches and we talked.

We talked about our families and what we liked to do and then we got on to talking about books and he didn't look bored or change the subject. I found out that he was passionate about history like me – that's why he'd been so keen to see where his ancestors came from.

And then he kissed me.

'Oh Alice,' Zack breathed, after what seemed an eternity. 'Will you . . . can we . . . I'd like to think of you as my girl. Would that be OK with you?'

Was it OK? My heart soared and I felt I could conquer Hitler single-handed. Suddenly the bomb sites, with their sprouting weeds and noisy kids playing at Germans versus Allies, seemed beautiful places because his feet had walked over them.

'I'd like that,' I whispered. 'A lot.'

Saying goodbye was the hardest thing. He had told all about the missions he flew night after night into occupied territory. I knew what could happen; my dad had been doing the same thing the night he was shot down.

'Be careful,' I pleaded with him, as if he could somehow think himself out of danger. 'Will you write to me? Let me know you are safe?'

'Of course I will,' he said. 'What's your address?'

I began to reel it off to him and stopped. Suddenly I didn't want my mother to find out about Zack – not yet, anyway. She'd always been a bit funny about my friends – wanting to know if they were what she called 'suitable', and I was pretty sure that an American airman wouldn't be the sort of boyfriend she'd approve of.

'Write to me at 14 Victoria Street.' Vi's address. I'd have to square it with Vi and make her promise to keep quiet, but I could do that, even if it cost me a few sweet coupons. 'You will write?'

Zack nodded. 'Even if I can only send a single line on a postcard, I'll write every couple of days. I promise.'

And he did. Sometimes the card just said 'Safely back, love you always, Zack' and sometimes there was a bit more – about how much he was looking forward to seeing me again, or a hint of a surprise he'd got for me.

I wrote back, of course, long letters about anything and everything I could think of. I told him how much I missed him, gave him the lowdown on Vi's love life (which took at least two pages every time because she never stuck with the same guy for very long) and tried to make him laugh. I told him about the books I was reading, even copying big chunks on to the notepaper for him. Once, he sent me a card which said that my letters kept him going and he never flew without having one next to his skin.

I cried when I read that. Mum caught me sniffling and I was tempted to tell her about Zack. But I didn't – after what had happened when I got home the day Zack and I spent together, I knew that I had to keep him a secret.

Zack had left me at the corner of Vale Street and I'd sped home in order to get there before my mother got back from her afternoon shift at the station. I was lying on my bed, trying to look pale and sickly when the front door slammed and my mother's footsteps thudded up the stairs.

'Alice!' She flung open the bedroom door. 'And just what do you think you are doing?'

I held on to my tummy and rolled over.

'I was sick at work, Mum, and I had this awful pain and –'

'So sick that you decided to go gallivanting with some Yank? So much pain that you were seen holding his hand!'

My heart sank. I guess I should have known it would happen – round my way, everyone minded everyone else's business.

'I . . .'

'Don't make excuses!' she shouted. 'Lily Durrant saw you in Victoria Park – I have never been so ashamed in my whole life!'

'I didn't do anything wrong,' I protested.

'Nothing wrong? Shirking your work? Acting like a hussy with some soldier –'

'Airman,' I corrected her and instantly regretted it.

'They're even worse!'

She pulled me up off the bed.

'And what about Stanley?' she demanded.

'What about him?'

'There he is, fighting for his country, and there you are, his girlfriend . . .'

'Mum, I am not his girlfriend!'

'He thinks you are.'

'Well, that's his problem, isn't it?' I shouted.

'Well let me tell you this, young lady,' she went on. 'From now on, I'll be keeping a close eye on you. I don't ever want you behaving like this again – these Yanks may be on our side but they don't have our morals – them with their flashy ways and money coming out of their ears.'

I didn't argue. There wasn't any point. After all, I hadn't a clue how long it would be before I could see Zack again and I didn't want my mother's anger to spoil what had been the best day of my entire life.

'Oh well, in future you will have to read the cards at my house and hide them under my mattress!' Vi grinned when I told her about my mother's reaction. 'Mind you, it will cost you . . .'

'Not more sweet rations?' I moaned.

''No, silly,' she replied. 'You have to promise to let me be your bridesmaid!'

'Give over!' I laughed, but inside I was glowing. Was it really possible that one day we'd be married and I'd go to live in America and be rich beyond my wildest dreams? Everyone knew that Americans lived in huge houses and were rolling in money – you only had to see the way the GIs flung their cash around to know that.

Twice after that Zack sent postcards to say he had some leave coming up and asking me to meet him – and twice they were followed by cards saying all leave had been cancelled. I would be so excited – and then spend the next few days crying all over Vi and saying that we were fated never to meet again.

And because I couldn't talk to Mum about it, I got into more trouble.

'What's the matter with you, moping about like a wet weekend?' she would snap. 'Think yourself lucky to be alive and put a smile on your face.'

Every time I went out to the cinema with Pam or Vi, she would give me one of her long looks and start issuing instructions. 'Now just you behave in a proper manner,' she would say, usually in front of my friends which was so embarrassing. 'No being silly with boys, do you hear me?'

'Yes, Mum,' I would reply meekly. There was only one guy I wanted to be silly with, as she put it. I would sit staring at the screen, imagining his hand in mine and his breath on my cheek, and often tears would roll down my face and I would have to pretend to my friends that the movie was making me cry.

We didn't have a telephone, of course, and he couldn't give me his number at the airbase so I had no choice but to wait.

And wait.

But then, just as I was sinking into the deepest depths of despair, the card I had been dreaming of arrived.

'Twenty-four-hour leave Saturday – meet me St Paul's Cathedral steps twelve noon for history fix! Love, Zack.'

My heart raced. St Paul's – that was three tube stops away and besides, I didn't finish work till one on Saturday. I couldn't risk skiving off again but no way would I give up the chance to be with Zack. Mum was on early shift at the station and would be home for lunch; but I'd think of something. I'd have to.

I scribbled a card in reply.

'I'll be there at two – please wait! Love you, Alice.'

I ran all the way to the post office and kissed the card as I slipped it into the mailbox.

'Alice! Oh, Alice!'

I spun round to see my mother lurching her way down the road, dodging the few kids who were playing in the street. I was terrified that she'd seen me at the post box and would start asking questions about who I was writing to. But as she drew closer, panting and red in the face, I realised that she was crying.

'Mum, what is it?'

She stopped, gasping for breath. 'It's Alf,' she said. 'Stanley's brother – he's been killed.'

My blood ran cold. 'No,' I heard myself say. 'No!'

Suddenly, life seemed to hang by a thread – even more than it had done before. It was as if everything lovely or special was about to be snatched away, as if happiness was just an illusion, a sort of prelude to being miserable for ever. An image of Zack swam before my eyes – Zack lying dead in the burned-out shell of an aeroplane. I felt more frightened than ever before.

But then Mum said something which lifted my heart, even though I knew I shouldn't feel that way.

'Of course, poor Dorothy can't go into work tomorrow, so I said I'd cover for her at the butcher's, in the afternoon. I don't like leaving you on your own for so long, but . . .'

'That's OK, Mum!' I smiled, trying to look sympathetic and understanding rather than elated. 'I'll be fine, honestly.'

If only I'd left it at that. If only I hadn't gone babbling on.

'Actually, I was thinking of spending the afternoon with Pam,' I said. 'She's helping down at the rest centre and . . .'

'Now that's lovely, dear,' Mum said. 'Thinking of others instead of yourself. Bless you!'

And with that she kissed the top of my head and slipped her hand in mine.

'You're a good girl, really,' she said, as if it came as something of a surprise to her. 'You'll make a lovely little wife and mother, you know.'

I was feeling too guilty to protest so I just smiled.

'Stanley's going to need you,' she went on. 'He's getting compassionate leave – he'll be home in a few days.'

I said nothing. I was too busy thinking about what to wear on Saturday.

It was such a different day from the first one we had spent together. For one thing, it was pouring with rain; by the time I reached the steps of St Paul's, my bare legs were spattered with dirt from the passing traffic. There was no sign of Zack on the steps, but I reasoned that in that kind of weather, he would have gone inside.

Ten minutes later, I was on the verge of tears. He wasn't there. He'd given up on me. What if he hadn't received my card? What if he thought I'd stood him up? What if . . . ?

'Alice.'

I wheeled around and gasped. It was Zack – but not the Zack of three months ago. His face was drawn and grey; his eyes dull.

'Oh Alice.' He drew me towards him, buried his face in my hair and held me as if he never wanted to let go. 'I'm sorry I'm late. I've been walking around. Everything's been so awful . . .'

'What is it?' I pulled back gently and looked into his eyes.

'Remember Brad?' he said. 'The tall guy who introduced us – the one who danced with your friend?'

I nodded.

'Dead!' He almost spat the word out. 'I saw it . . . he fell out of the sky . . . he didn't have a chance.'

'Oh, Zack, I'm so sorry, I . . .'

'He died on his birthday – his twentieth birthday,' he went on. 'What a goddamn waste!'

I didn't know what to say so I just squeezed his hand and waited.

'Look at them all!' He waved his hand around the great space of St Paul's, towards the stone tombs and the statues and the brass plates set into the floor of the aisle. 'Dead, dead, dead – and all remembered! But Brad – fifty years from now, who's going to care about him? And all the others?'

'People will,' I told him. 'People won't ever forget this war. How could they?'

Zack shook his head and sighed. 'Things get better and folk forget,' he said dully. 'We won't, though, will we?'

I shook my head. 'Never,' I whispered. 'Never, ever.'

He nodded slowly.

'Anyway,' he said briskly, 'enough of that. What shall we do? I don't have very long – something big's coming up and I've got to get back by nine.'

'Something big?' My voice wavered and I was filled

with a feeling of doom. I gripped his hand as if I would never let it go.

'Oh, probably something of nothing!' His lips were smiling, but his eyes didn't meet mine.

'I don't care what we do!' I gabbled. 'I just want to be with you and pretend . . .'

I stopped. How could I say that I wanted to pretend it would last forever? Nothing did. I thought of my dad, home on leave one day and shot from the sky the next. I thought about Dora, the funniest girl in my class, dead at fifteen.

And then I thought about Zack, taking off into the night sky, heading for Germany . . .

I wouldn't let myself think any further. I couldn't bear to think of him anywhere but close to me.

'Hey, what's with the gloomy face?' he teased. 'Will these cheer you up?' He shoved a package into my hands.

'Stockings!' I couldn't believe my eyes. Real nylon stockings! 'Thank you, thank you!' I hugged him. 'I'll save them for the next time you come!'

'Now there's an incentive!' he teased. 'And there's this too!'

It was a book. *History of the Sioux*. I stared at it. I didn't want to admit that I hadn't a clue what *Sioux* meant.

'It's about some North American Indians,' he explained. 'I brought it with me from home. You said you liked history and . . . but if you don't want it . . .'

'It's brilliant!' I told him. 'I'll treasure it forever.'

I remember every moment of that afternoon. We went

to the cinema to see *Gone With the Wind*. I'd seen it before, which was just as well, because neither of us took much notice of what was happening on the screen.

It was when the newsreels came on that Zack began to tense up. He would watch the screen for a few minutes and then turn and hold me close to him, squeezing me so tightly that I could hardly breathe.

'When this war is over,' he whispered into my ear, 'I'm going somewhere with big open spaces and peace and quiet, and I'm never going to leave it – ever.'

I felt sick. Which would be worse – knowing he was in mortal danger day after day, or having him thousands of miles away from me across the ocean?

'But first,' he said, taking my hand and kissing my fingers one by one, 'I'm coming back for you.'

'You mean . . . ?'

'I mean, Alice Jupp, that since I'm head over heels in love with you, I won't be going anywhere without you.'

After that, we didn't even pretend to be watching the film.

'I can't bear this!' I was crying and clinging to Zack. I knew his friend was coming to meet him in ten minutes for the drive back to Ridgewell. 'When will I see you again?'

'I don't know, sweetheart,' he replied gently. 'None of us think about tomorrow any more – we just try to get through today. But if I have any tomorrows –'

'Don't say that!' I shouted. 'You will, you have to . . . I couldn't bear . . .'

'. . . I want all my tomorrows with you,' he said. 'I know you're only eighteen and . . .'

I felt colour rush to my cheeks and buried my face in his jacket to hide my embarrassment.

'But will you wait?' His voice was so soft I could hardly hear the words.

'Yes – yes, of course I will.'

'I'll take you back to the States and you can go to college and then set up a school in Wolf Creek and teach all the local kids about British history!' he smiled. 'How would that be?'

'Heaven!'

He turned as the roar of an approaching motorbike broke the moment.

'It's Grant,' he said. 'I've got to go.'

He gave me one last lingering kiss.

'Keep writing, angel,' he begged. 'Your letters are what keep me going. Those and the ones from home. I've told them about you.'

'You have?'

'Here . . .' He fumbled in his pocket and pulled out a slip of paper. As he did so a coin fell on to the pavement. 'It's my folks' address,' he explained, turning and gesturing to Grant to wait by the corner. 'If anything happens to me . . .'

The words made me feel sick.

'You dropped this,' I murmured, bending down to pick

up the coin and brushing the tears from my eyes. I didn't want to let him down, have his last memory of me spoiled by my crying. There would be time enough for that later on.

'Keep it,' he said. 'Whatever it is. I never did get the hang of your English coins.'

'A shilling,' I told him. 'I can't keep it . . .'

'Please. I want you to.' He took my hand and raised it to his lips. 'Keep it with you every day until I come back to collect it. Promise?'

'I promise,' I whispered. 'I won't let it out of my sight.'

Grant revved the motorbike engine and gestured at the watch on his wrist.

'Time to go,' he sighed. 'I love you, Alice.'

'I love you too.' Despite all my efforts I choked on the words. 'Keep safe for me.'

'. . . and remember, I'll want that shilling back sooner or later!'

'You bet!' I waved and blew kisses until the motorbike rounded the corner and disappeared. And then, ignoring the gazes of the passers-by I cried as I had never cried before.

It wasn't until I reached the Underground station that I realised how late it was. A quater-past seven! – I wouldn't be home till eight at the earliest and my mother would be furious. I prayed that she had not checked up on me.

The train seemed to take forever and when we did get to the station, I had to push my way past all the people who were coming down the stairs with their blankets and pillows, ready to spend the night on the platform to escape the air raids. We hadn't been getting so many as before – but even Mum and I slept in the cupboard under the stairs when we thought things might get nasty. They said that if your house got hit, the last thing to collapse would be the staircase.

As I climbed the stairs, a woman grabbed my arm.

'You don't want to go up there, kid,' she insisted. 'The sirens have just gone off – them damned Huns are on their way again!'

'I have to go,' I told her. 'My mum'll be worried.'

'Suit yourself,' she sighed. 'Johnny, you do that once more and I'll have your guts for . . .'

I gave her little boy a sympathetic wink and hurried on.

But when I got to the top of the stairs, one of the air-raid wardens grabbed my arm.

'Hang on, love,' he said. 'It's started.'

It was a bad one. I heard the bomb singing through the air and the massive explosion that seemed only feet away. And then another.

One would think we would all have got used to the bombing after three and a half years – but we hadn't. With every whine, every explosion, you could see the colour draining from people's faces as they wondered what they would find when they got out.

I sat there, clutching my shilling and trying to blot out the noise by rerunning every second of the afternoon in my head. But somehow, all I could see in my mind's eye was Zack up there in the sky, with gunfire raging all around him.

'God, if you keep him safe, I'll do anything – anything you want.' Silently I said the words, turning the shilling over and over in my hand like some lucky charm.

Eventually, we heard the drone of the Messerschmitt engines receding as they flew mercilessly on to their next target.

It seemed for ever before the 'All Clear' sounded. I belted down the road, across the main street and around the corner towards our house . . . and stopped.

Half my street had disappeared.

They told me at the hospital that Mum wouldn't have known a thing. Instant, it would have been, they told me. One minute she was running down the street, and the next . . .

It was left to the neighbours to tell me why she was out in the first place.

'She was heading for the rest centre,' Dorothy said later, her face streaked with tears. 'She told me you were there helping out – and that first bomb sounded like it fell really close by. She just screamed your name and started running . . .'

That's when I knew it was all my fault. I had killed my mother.

The rest of them might be blaming a German bomb but

I knew different. If I hadn't lied to her, hadn't pretended to be somewhere I wasn't, my mother would still have been alive.

I don't remember much more about that day, except one thing.

After my trip to the mortuary, Dorothy took me to her house, one of the few that remained standing on the street, one that didn't have windows blown in or doors hanging off their hinges.

She made me tea, and gently took the pitiful little bag of Mum's things that the hospital had handed me. Her watch, her glasses and the pearl necklace Dad gave her when I was born.

'And what's that, lovey?' Dorothy asked gently as I sobbed. 'What's that you're holding?'

She prised my fingers open, and there, in my hot, sticky palm, lay the shilling I had been clutching ever since I had parted from Zack – what seemed a lifetime ago.

'Well, well . . .' she sighed. 'Your mum said she'd forgotten to give you back a bit out of your wages – really worried, she was, saying that you were such a good girl and it was only fair you should have a bit to spend. I guess she had it with her to give you when . . .'

Her voice trailed off.

I swallowed.

'You'll be wanting to keep that by you, love,' Dorothy went on. 'A little memento, like.'

She didn't know it, and at the time I was too shocked to make sense of it, but on the very day that my lies had killed my mother, Dorothy had made it easy for me to start another one.

'I will,' I sobbed, 'I'll never, ever let it out of my sight.'

And I never did.

Dorothy took me into her home. Mine was still standing – although most of the windows had been blown in – but I couldn't face being there on my own.

In fact, I couldn't face anything. Each day was a blur, one melting into another. Vi did everything she could; she came to see me every day, and tried to cheer me up, but to be honest, I couldn't relate to anyone or anything.

The funeral came and went; Gran, Mum's mother, said I could go and live with her in Bolton if I wanted, and then spent the next hour telling everyone that it would probably be the death of her and how if I came I'd have to pay my way and keep out from under her feet.

There was no way I'd have gone – with her, or with anyone else. I was staying put in Bethnal Green. I had to be where Zack could get to me the very instant he had the chance.

Dorothy gave me Alf's bedroom. I protested but she was adamant.

'He was that fond of you, lovey,' she said with tears in her eyes. 'And besides, what's the point of me keeping it as a shrine? He's gone now but you're here, and you must have it till you get yourself sorted.'

We moved a few bits of furniture down the street from my old home. The moment I stepped into the hallway, all the pain and guilt came flooding back. I could see Mum in every corner of every room – scrubbing carrots at the kitchen sink, doing the mending in the old rocking chair by the hearth, stomping up the stairs to tick me off for lying in bed too late. On the floor of the kitchen the clock lay smashed by the impact of the bomb. It had stopped at 7.21 p.m. Why hadn't I got an earlier train? Why hadn't I told her the truth? I felt as if I was going out of my mind.

It was the thought of Zack that kept me going. The day after Mum's death, I wrote to him, a long rambling letter stained with tears, telling him how guilty I felt, telling him that I felt so alone now that both Mum and Dad were dead, and saying that he was the only person left in the entire world that I cared about.

'Write back quickly,' I begged him. 'I'm so miserable.'

I thought he would reply by return, but no letter came. Every morning I watched for the postman and every morning I was disappointed. Dorothy's wireless was never switched off and whenever I heard about bombing raids over Germany, or crashed aeroplanes in the Channel, I would hold my breath until I heard that they came from anywhere other than Ridgewell airbase.

Every night I read the book he'd given me, sniffing the pages in the hope of catching a whiff of his scent, happy that my fingers were tracing the words his fingers had traced.

And still the postman walked by the house.

And, in the meantime, Stanley came home.

I suppose it was inevitable really – that we should turn to one another for comfort. After all, we were both still kids. He may have been rising nineteen, but once he was inside 11 Edith Street, he was just a boy mourning his adored big brother.

'It was so awful,' he told me over and over again. 'I passed right by the stretcher-bearers – they were carrying this poor bloke, missing both legs and blood pumping out like a fountain. And I didn't even know it was Alf.'

I tried not to picture the scene. Stanley swallowed hard. 'Then something made me look back,' he went on, 'and I saw the tattoo on his arm. Only don't tell Mum!'

Suddenly he was the kid brother keeping a secret. 'She'd have gone mad, knowing he'd had it done.' He smiled. 'He met this girl, see – Francine, her name was – and in a mad moment, he had this heart tattooed with F and A in the middle.' He sighed helplessly and buried his head in his hands.

'Not that it matters now, does it?' he blurted out. 'Nothing matters any more . . . except you.' He grabbed my hand and was about to pull me towards him.

'Stan, there's something you should know,' I began. 'You see, while you were away . . .'

'Oh Alice, I'm sorry! Here's me going on and on and I

haven't said so much as two words about your poor mum.'

'It's OK, I . . .'

'No, it's not OK! You must miss her dreadfully.'

I nodded, reaching for the shilling that was always in my pocket.

'I keep seeing her face,' I wept. 'They'd covered her with a sheet because she was so badly blown about – but her face – it was just like she was asleep. I wish . . .' I stopped.

'I'll look after you,' Stanley promised. 'When I get back from the war –'

'Stan, there's something I ought to tell you . . .' I faltered. I didn't know how to put it. I turned the coin over and over in my hand.

Stanley reached out as if to take it from me, and I flinched as though he had hit me.

'Is that the shilling Mum was telling me about?' he asked gently. 'The one your mum had with her to give you when she . . . when the bomb fell?'

It was easier to nod. Easier than telling the truth. After all, why hurt him now, when after three days he'd be back in the midst of gunfire and bombs and maybe end up like his brother? So I nodded.

'Tell you what,' Stanley said, 'how would it be if I made it into a necklace for you? Or a bracelet? Then you could wear it all the time and there'd be no fear of you losing it.'

I stared at him. 'You would . . . I mean, how could . . . ?'

He laughed. 'Easy! Dad's old soldering iron and a bit of chain – it'd be done in no time!'

He made it that very afternoon.

'There!' he said when it was done. 'Now you'll have a bit of your mum with you all the time.' And then he pulled me close to him.

'Allypally,' he said, using the nickname he'd given me when I was about six years old. 'You'll wait, won't you? I mean, this war won't last forever, and then I'll be home and you and me . . .'

'I . . .'

'I want to care for you, Ally,' he whispered. 'I want to look after you – always.'

His face was bright red, and he looked so vulnerable.

'Say you'll wait,' he pleaded.

'I'll be here when you get home,' I said. 'Where else would I be?'

I told myself it wasn't a lie – after all, I wouldn't be going off with Zack the very second the war ended and by then, Stanley would have grown out of his crush and everything would be OK.

'That's all right, then.' He was grinning. 'Now put this on.' He slipped the bracelet over my wrist.

'I know it's a memento of your mum,' he said, 'but when you look at it – well, perhaps there's one other person you could think of as well?'

This time I didn't have to lie. 'Oh yes,' I smiled. 'There's someone I'll be thinking of every moment of the day.'

As soon as the words were out I realised how cruel I was. But I still let Stanley think that I meant him.

Zack didn't write back. Eight weeks went by and I didn't hear a word.

I was sure that he hated me – hated me for being a liar and killing my mum. Night after night I would lie awake imagining him reading my letter and deciding that he never wanted to see me again.

Nevertheless, I nagged Vi senseless, making her check and double check that her mum hadn't picked up some mail meant for me and hidden it somewhere.

'Alice, you have to accept it,' Vi sighed. 'He's a guy – he was up for some fun and now he's moved on. They do it – especially the Yanks.'

'Not Zack!' I yelled at her. 'You don't understand – he and I, we were special.'

'Well, maybe he's – well, you know – bought it,' she murmured. Vi was full of the jargon she had picked up from the movies. 'Write to the airbase and find out.'

That's when I remembered the piece of paper he had given me when we parted, the one with his parents' address scribbled on it.

'I'll write to them,' I exclaimed, poking Vi in my excitement. 'They'll know where Zack is and they'll tell him to get in touch.'

Vi gave me a pitying look and opened her mouth to speak, but clearly thought better of it.

The letter never got written. I hunted through the pockets of my coat but the scrap of paper had gone.

'Oh, lovey, I don't know,' Dorothy sighed when I asked

her about it. 'I gave the coat a good clean when you got home from the hospital that night – it was all grimy and dusty . . .'

'You shouldn't have done it without asking me!' I shouted. 'It's my property.'

Poor Dorothy looked mortified. 'Well, I . . .'

'I'm sorry,' I said bursting into tears. 'It's just that . . .'

'Just what, ducks?'

'Nothing,' I said. 'It doesn't matter.'

The war did end, eventually. I was eighteen by then, and I hadn't heard from Zack for nearly two years. Vi told me that either he was dead, and I was wasting my time pining for him, or else he had forgotten me, which amounted to the same thing.

I thought she was right about him forgetting but I knew he wasn't dead. I don't know how I knew; I just felt it deep inside me.

And I still thought about him every single day. I was thinking of him the night Stanley proposed.

'Mum says we can have the spare room,' he said eagerly, 'and now Dad's gone, it's up to me to build up the drapery business. I'll make something of myself, Alice, honestly I will. Say you love me. Say you'll marry me.'

I think if he'd left it at that I would have had the courage to turn him down. But then he took my hand again and looked deep into my eyes.

'Your mum would have wanted it, Alice – it would have made her so happy. I guess she's up there now, looking down on us and holding her breath, just like I am.'

Maybe it was the months and months of loneliness, or maybe I just wanted to believe that by saying yes to Stanley I could wipe out the guilt of causing my mother's death, but suddenly it seemed like the sensible thing to do.

'Yes, Stanley Turnbull, I'll marry you,' I said. But even then, I never said I loved him.

And in all the years we were together, there was never to be a single day when I didn't think about Zack.

EMILY

June

FOR SEVERAL MOMENTS after Lally finishes her story, no one speaks. Mum has walked over to the window and is staring out on to the street, and I keep fiddling with a teaspoon, trying to think of the right thing to say.

'You still love him.' It's Mum who speaks first and it isn't a question – it's a statement.

Lally nods.

'And now you've got this mad idea about going to live in America . . . to meet up with a man you haven't seen in nearly sixty years.'

'Oh, but I have seen him,' Lally replies. 'Many times.'

'So *that's* why you keep going to America for holidays!' I exclaim. 'That is so romantic!'

Mum gasps. 'Are you telling me . . . those holidays – they were *all* to visit him?'

Lally nods. 'In 1948, I got a letter.' She sighs, misty-eyed. 'In fact, I'll go and get it. You can read it for yourselves.'

She heaves herself out of her armchair and is heading up the stairs when the doorbell rings.

'Get that, one of you!' she calls. 'I'll be down in a tick.'

Mum gives an exasperated sigh and stomps her way to the door.

'We're looking for Alice Turnbull,' I hear a man say.

'And who are you?' The suspicion in my mother's voice carries right through to the sitting room.

'Doug and Phyllis Manders,' pipes up a female voice. 'We are buying her daughter's house.'

'I was going to tell you – and then, what with losing the bracelet and everything else,' Lally explains apologetically, 'it just went out of my head.'

'I can't believe it!' Mum gasps. 'I thought it would take weeks to sell the place!'

'Clever, aren't I?' Lally grins. 'Mind you, I do think you should have taken them over to your house right away, especially since they had been sitting outside the place for nearly an hour hoping you'd be back.'

'I suppose I should have,' Mum sighs, 'but I did have other things on my mind, if you recall.' She glances ruefully at Lally. 'Anyway, they were quite happy to come back tomorrow,' she adds, '. . . assuming I'm still selling.'

'What do you mean?' Lally asks.

'You said Emily and I could move in with you, but now you're talking about swanning off to the States and . . .' She sounds close to tears.

'That won't make any difference!' Lally replies briskly. 'It'll be good to know the house is in safe hands – in fact, you can have it lock, stock and barrel, provided you agree that if anything goes wrong, I can come back and . . .'

'Ah, so you admit it might well go wrong!'

'No,' Lally says calmly, fingering her bare wrist. 'But

contrary to what you think of me, I am not totally senile. I'm taking sensible precautions.'

My mother slumps down into a chair and rubs her eyes. 'I just can't get my head round this, Ma.' She sighs. 'First Emily, now you . . .'

'Well,' Lally says. 'It's half-past four – suppose Emily makes us a cup of tea and . . .'

'Half-past four!' I leap up and stare at my watch. 'I've got to go!'

'Go?' My mother and Lally chorus together. 'Go where?'

'I promised to meet . . .' I bit my lip, '. . . some friends from school – on the seafront. It won't take long.'

To my amazement, my mother doesn't utter one word of protest. She simply stands up and grabs her handbag.

'I'll drop you off,' she offers. 'I need to be alone for a bit anyway.'

'But Lally was going to show you the letter and –'

'It'll keep,' Lally interrupts with a smile. 'It's been in my drawer for over fifty years. Another day won't matter.'

❧

I think I might have a boyfriend.

I'm not sure, but if a hug, a quick kiss and a promise of a late evening phone call are how love affairs start, I think I might be on the way.

I mean, I'm not likely to get Rufus and besides, Hugo notices me and Rufus doesn't.

I'm not sure how it happened. I keep re-running this afternoon in my head to work it out.

'I thought you weren't coming,' Hugo said after I belted across Brunswick Lawns and into the café.

'Sorry,' I panted. 'Things got a bit complicated.' Master of understatement, me.

'Well, I can't stop long,' he said. 'I got you a lemonade, but if you want tea, coffee . . .'

I shook my head. 'Lemonade's fine, thanks. So what was it you wanted to ask me?'

Hugo thrust a big brown envelope in my hands.

'Take a look,' he ordered.

I opened the flap and pulled out a pile of photos. And gasped out loud.

There I was, caught in mid-flight as I jumped off the wall at Viki's party; there I was, gazing up into Rufus's eyes as he pecked my cheek. There was even one of me looking slightly sick as I staggered into the garden. But the best one of all was of me dancing on top of the wall, arms in the air, head thrown back and a big grin on my face.

'Wow!' I breathed. 'They're amazing.'

Hugo nodded. 'And now look at these,' he said, passing me a transparent plastic sleeve.

'Boring!' I sighed. These were just the usual – me standing by the tennis net holding my trophy, me reaching for a baseline ball, me shaking hands with the umpire. I handed them back to Hugo.

'What I want to know is, will you let me use them?' he asked, sipping his drink. 'Well, not the tennis ones – they belong to the *Evening Argus* anyway, so you've got no choice, but the others.'

'What for?'

'There's this competition that Southern Newspapers run each year – Most Promising New Journalist,' he explained eagerly. 'You submit a feature, about a thousand words, with pictures on any topic of your choice – and the winner gets fifteen hundred pounds.'

'Wow!'

'But that's not the most important bit,' he said. 'It's the most terrific leg up you can have – win that and loads of newspapers will offer you a job.'

'But I thought you didn't want to be a sports journalist.'

'I don't!'

'So . . .'

'Emily, it's a question of getting myself noticed, OK? Once people accept I'm good, I can get on with doing what I really want.'

'Which is?'

'In the end, I want to be a foreign correspondent,' he said. 'For one of the nationals.'

'You mean, in war zones and stuff?'

He shrugged. 'Wherever,' he said. 'I want to make people see what's going on in the world, but I want to write about it in ways that everyone, not just the highly intellectual, can understand. I want to be in the thick of it, see for myself and then tell it how it is.'

'Maybe you're right,' I heard myself say, 'maybe we do have more in common than I thought.' If you ask me, I'm more dangerous sober than drunk. I gulped down some lemonade and prayed that he hadn't heard.

He had.

'What do you mean?' he asked, in that same excited tone.

'Nothing.'

'Oh come on . . .'

'I want to work with an aid agency, helping refugees,' I mumbled, staring out at the yachts bobbing about on the horizon.'In Africa probably.'

'That's brilliant!' Hugo exclaimed. 'So you've decided against the tennis, then?'

I sighed. 'I have, but my mother, and Felix and my coach . . .'

Suddenly he gripped my shoulders. 'Do it, Emily,' he stressed. 'You can't spend your life dancing to someone else's tune. My dad wanted me to follow him into the family business – but the thought of a lifetime doing other people's accounts . . .' He pulled a face and shuddered.

'But what if I don't make it to uni?' I began. 'I'd have wasted . . .'

'If you don't try, you'll never know,' he said. 'And then you'll spend the rest of your life wondering about what might have been.'

I sighed, and thought of Lally and what she must have been thinking each day as she cooked, cleaned and wrote her history essays.

'Yes, but if I don't do the tennis I might wonder about that,' I reasoned.

'So – you have to make a choice. Look!' He thrust the photos back in my hand.

'Which Emily is the real one? That . . .' He stabbed a finger at me holding my silver cup. 'Or that?' he asked, waving the party pictures in my face.

'Or . . .' he went on before I had a chance to comment, 'is the real Emily still hidden somewhere inside her?'

He blushed and looked away.

'I guess I'm still looking for the real me, in a way,' I muttered, and then wished I'd kept my mouth shut until I could think of something more sophisticated and clever to say.

'I don't suppose,' he said quietly, turning his empty glass round and round in his hands, 'that you'd let me help you look?'

He turned and took my hand. 'I'm not very good with girls,' he said, looking flustered. 'But you're not like other girls. I can talk to you.'

'Gosh!' I butted in. 'A girl with a brain – whatever next?'

He grinned. 'I didn't mean it like that,' he added, 'I just meant – well, would you like to come out sometime?'

'Yes please.' Charlie would have gone ballistic; she says you must never sound enthusiastic.

That's when he kissed me – just a quick one on the top of my head, but nevertheless . . .

'I have to go,' he said after a few moments. 'And you still haven't said yes.'

'I just did!' I protested.

'Not about that, silly,' he replied, grinning. 'About the

photos – can I use them for the competition entry?'

I hesitated. 'Well – if you really think it'll help . . . but it won't go in the paper . . . Felix said I mustn't talk to the press and . . .'

'I guess they'd only use them if I won,' he said. 'And by then, you will have told Felix that you don't want the scholarship anyway, right?'

'I suppose.' I nodded. 'OK then.'

He gave me a huge hug.

'Thank you!' he breathed. 'Now I must dash – I've written the feature already but it needs a bit of tidying up, and I have to get the editor's approval before I send it off. I'll call you tonight – on your mobile. Is that OK?'

So I'm waiting. I hope he rings soon. For one thing, I want to hear his voice, but more importantly, it will give me an excuse to escape Mum's incessant nagging.

She started the very moment I got home.

'Now Emily, about this ridiculous idea of yours . . .'

It went on and on, but I kept hearing Hugo's words in my head, and remembering Lally's story.

'Mum, I've made up my mind,' I told her. 'I'm staying on at school, OK?'

I thought I had better soften her up a bit so I gave her a hug. 'I promise I'll work really hard and make you proud of me and –'

'And what am I going to tell Felix? And Judy?'

Judy's my coach at the local club and I admit she's a pretty fierce woman.

'I'll tell them,' I said boldly.

'You do that!' she retorted and stormed upstairs.

Terrific. How's that for parental support?

I know she thinks I'm being an idiot, but I know I'm doing the right thing . . . at least I think I am. I just wish I could be completely sure.

He didn't ring. I stayed awake till midnight. I slept with my mobile on the bedside table, and I had the volume turned all the way up, but he didn't ring.

This morning I even did what Charlie said you must never do – I tried to phone him. I flipped my phone menu through to Last Calls Received, sure that his number would be there from when he phoned me on Sunday morning.

'WITHHELD,' it said.

We're not allowed to have our mobiles switched on in school, so I went to the loo about a dozen times during the day to see whether he'd left a message.

He hadn't.

If it hadn't been for Viki, I'd have been really down in the dumps about it.

'Hey, Em,' she called as we filed into the cafeteria for lunch, 'how's the love life?'

'What love life?' I asked, wishing that I didn't blush so easily.

'*What love life?*' she mimicked. 'As if you didn't know. Hugo Fraser, silly. He practically begged me to let him have those pictures from the party.'

I tried to look cool about it. 'It's only for a competition . . .' I began.

'Oh yeah, yeah!' She laughed. 'I got that story too. But if you ask me, he's besotted! Has he been in touch?'

I nodded. 'I saw him yesterday,' I admitted.

'And?'

'And nothing,' I retorted. 'Well, not yet.'

'Aha!' Viki cried. 'Well, let me know how you get on – after all, if it hadn't been for my photographic genius, you might never have got it together.'

At this rate, we won't be doing that. It's four o'clock and he hasn't rung.

What's more I've got two hours of tennis coaching ahead of me and I'm not in the mood. It's pointless. There's nothing for it – I'll just have to make Judy see things my way.

I can't go on like this.

My mother is waiting for me in the car. She's reading the paper and she has a face like thunder.

'Did those people like the house, Mum?' I ask sweetly, fastening my seat belt. I've always found that my mother is flummoxed when I'm charming. Until today, that is.

'Never mind the house!' she snaps. 'What the hell do you mean by this?'

She slaps the newspaper on to my lap.

'Page 11. Well, go on, look!'

I flick over the pages of the *Evening Argus*.

'How could you do something so stupid?' My mother spits out the words and stabs at the page.

My heart sinks.

'*All in a day's play!*' The headline glares up at me. But there's worse to come. In the middle of the page are two pictures – one of me hitting the winning shot last Saturday, and the other of me leaping off the wall at the party, one shoe flying through the air in front of me, my arms outstretched towards Hugo.

The pictures are captioned '*Match Point!*' and '*Break Point?*'

'*In the first of an occasional series on headline-hitting teenagers, Hugo Fraser looks at the two sides of local tennis superstar, Emily Driver.*'

'Mum, I didn't know, honestly!' I stammer. 'I would never have agreed . . .'

'Agreed? You mean . . . you knew about this?'

I swallow hard.

'I meant that you could have broken your leg, fooling around like that, leaping off that wall! I never for one moment dreamed that you had anything to do with all this drivel being printed in the paper!'

'I didn't – I mean, he said it was for a competition . . .'

'You've spoken to this Fraser guy about this? How? When?'

She turns on the ignition and revs the engine.

'He was at Viki's party and we got talking and . . .'

'And that,' she shouted, gesturing to the paper, 'is the result. Go on, read it. Read the lot.'

I scan the page.

'*Emily Driver . . . one of the country's most promising players . . . partied the night away . . . wild child . . . but mention tennis, a curtain comes down . . .*'

When I see Hugo Fraser, I'll wring his neck.

'*Is this another case of force-fed youngsters . . . are they all so anxious to please their parents, their coaches . . . are we pushing our youngsters too hard? After all, it's a game, isn't it? Emily – is she Driver or driven?*'

'I'll kill him!' The words that have been swimming around in my head are suddenly on my lips.

'You know what this means, don't you?' growls my mother. She turns the wheel and pulls out into the traffic. 'This story has blown any chance of Felix taking you seriously. I wouldn't be surprised if he refused to have you . . .'

'Mum, I've already told you a dozen times,' I butt in. 'I'm not taking up the scholarship. So it doesn't matter, does it?'

She doesn't say a word until we reach the tennis club car park. Then she turns to me, and I see that her eyes are full of tears.

'You mean it, don't you?' she says.

I nod, not trusting myself to speak.

'Well thanks, Emily. Thank you for letting me waste the best years of my life on you! Thank you for nothing!'

In the end, I didn't have my tennis lesson. It's hard to keep your eye on the ball when you keep bursting into tears. Mum's words kept echoing in my head and Judy's stern glower didn't help.

'When I think of the dozens of pupils I've had who would have worked their socks off for an opportunity like you've got . . .'

By the time she had finished I felt even worse than before.

I'll never forgive Hugo – he promised that he wouldn't print stuff and he lied. To think I actually believed for a moment that we could be friends – or more. Some friend.

He said we had a lot in common; well, he was wrong. I would never *ever* treat a mate like that. He's scum.

❧

On Mondays, we always go to supper with Lally after coaching. Mum has been tight lipped and silent all the way here; each time I try to make conversation she just answers me with monosyllables.

'Did those people see the house, Mum?'

'Yes.'

'Did they like it?'

'Apparently.'

'Are they going to buy it?'

A shrug of the shoulders. I give up.

I so much want to ask her if she really meant that she felt I'd wasted her life, but I don't dare. I couldn't bear to hear her say it again.

Lally's waiting at the door and she's got a copy of the evening paper in her hand.

'Emily! Have you seen this?'

I nod, silently cursing the fact that the whole mess is going to be up for discussion again.

'Wonderful pictures, darling – you look so happy! We must get some copies!'

'Ma!' My mother is up the path and at the door in an instant. 'Have you read it?'

Lally nods. 'Uh-huh. Clever slant, isn't it?'

'Oh, for goodness' sake!' Mum rips the paper from Lally's hand and hurls it on to the hall table. 'It's a disaster! Everything's a disaster!' And with that she bursts into tears.

'Oh, I don't see why,' Lally says calmly, beckoning us through to the dining room and opening the drinks cabinet. 'It isn't as if Emily was going to go through with the tennis academy idea, is it? . . . Sherry?'

My mother waves a hand dismissively but Lally pours two large schooners anyway.

'Did you find that letter, Lally?' I blurt out, desperate to change the subject. 'The one from Zack?'

Lally smiles. 'I did,' she confirms. 'It's on the coffee table.'

I pick up a faded, almost disintegrating sheet of airmail paper.

'*Dearest Alice*,' I read out loud. '*At last I can write to you – and I pray to God that this letter will find you. The day after we parted, I flew a mission and was shot down, taken prisoner and spent the rest of the war in a German POW hospital. Only got one hand now which is why this letter is a bit of a scrawl.*

'I prayed there would be a letter from you when I finally got back to Wolf Creek – but there was nothing. Please say you haven't forgotten me. I thought I gave you my folks' address but maybe you lost it. So I'm sending this to your friend Vi's house in the hope that she will pass it on. I love you, Alice – I pray you still love me. Your guy, Zack.'

'Lally!' I whisper. 'That is so romantic. So why didn't you go out to Montana there and then? The letter's dated February 2nd, 1946. You weren't married yet.'

Lally sighs. 'Look at the postmarks on the envelope,' she says.

There are three, each dated later than the next.

'He obviously posted it to Vi's house, but they had moved to Wolverhampton by then,' she explains. 'That old terrace was demolished after the war, so there was no one to forward it on.' She takes the envelope from me and looks at it lovingly.

'By the time it finally reached me, it was 1948 and I wasn't Alice Jupp any more; I was Alice Turnbull.'

'But you wrote to him.' Mum's expression tells me she knows the answer.

'Oh yes,' says Lally. 'By then, he'd given up on me – he'd married a girl from his own home town, and she was already pregnant with their son.'

'1948?' Mum's voice was brittle. 'I was born in 1948.'

Lally smiles. 'You were the light on my horizon,' she says, patting Mum's hand and planting a kiss on her cheek. 'The one thing that kept me going.'

The corner of Mum's mouth twitches but she is still

frowning. 'What about Daddy?'

'I was fond of Stanley, very fond,' replies Lally. 'But he was never the main love of my life. He couldn't be – Zack already held that place in my heart.'

'So what happened?' I ask, secretly thinking that the next time we had a bit of creative writing to do at school, I would have it sussed.

'Well,' Lally says, 'we went on writing. Oh, I know what you're thinking – I was a married woman, he was a married man – but it wasn't like that. We were friends – we wrote about our lives, our children, our dreams.'

She smiled to herself. 'I was bored – stuck at home all the time . . .'

'Bored!' Mum cries. 'You always had your head in a book, or you were writing an essay or researching some bizarre topic . . .'

She pauses, a look of recognition fleeting across her face. 'Those courses you did – The American Civil War, Shaker Art, The Myths of the North American Indians –'

Lally nods. 'Learning about the States made me feel closer to Zack,' she admits. 'Besides, I was an intelligent woman, I needed stimulation. Cooking, polishing, ironing, shopping . . . the tedium really got me down. I used to devour books from the library and write to Zack about what I was reading and then when I started doing voluntary work –'

'So all that time that you were playing the part of the do-gooder, you were flirting with a married man!' Mum interjects.

Lally looks pained.

'You make it sound as if I were having a rampant affair with Zack,' she protests. 'We only wrote letters. Well . . . until 1971 when your father died.'

'And then?' Mum asks.

Lally takes a deep breath. 'The following year, I started having my holidays in America, remember?' she confesses. 'You'd left home, I was a free agent. I always spent those holidays with Zack.'

'So his wife had died too?' Mum asks, frowning.

'No.'

'But . . .'

'She was an invalid,' Lally goes on. 'She had a bad riding accident when their son was ten years old – she was in a wheelchair and suffered brain damage – the two of them never really had a life together after that.'

She looks pleadingly at my mother.

'We didn't do anyone any harm, Ruth – we had just two weeks a year together instead of the lifetime we'd planned,' she murmured. 'A different place every time – never at his home, so his neighbours and friends wouldn't talk. He was so loyal to Cathy – his wife. He said he could never leave her – not with her in the state she was. And then, last year, she finally died.'

Mum looks pale and she keeps wringing her hands.

'If you hadn't had me,' she says, staring out of the window, 'would you have left Dad and gone off with Zack?'

'I have to be honest,' Lally admits. 'I might have done if Zack had asked me. But I did have you, and there was no way on earth that I was going to take you away from your father.'

She puts an arm on Mum's shoulder.

'I made a choice, Ruth, way before you were born. In my heart, I always thought Zack must be alive – I was sure that if he wasn't, I'd feel it right in there.' She pummelled her chest and sighed.

'But – and it's a big but – I didn't have the courage to go against what everyone else thought was best for my life. Mum was dead, Dorothy had taken me into her home and all her family wanted me to marry Stanley. So I did.'

'Oh Lally, that must have been so hard!' I breathe. I tried to imagine myself in fifty years' time. How would I feel about my decision? How different things are for me . . . and how similar!

'Emily, it was my choice. I made a conscious decision not to wait for him.'

She smiles. 'And let's face it, if I had waited, I wouldn't have had your mother and I wouldn't be your granny – who knows what might have happened?'

She winks at us both.

'Now, shall we all have some supper? And then when we have finished, I want to show you pictures of the place I'm going to be living.'

'It's no good, I can't eat.' Mum pushes her plate away. 'My head is spinning, what with everything . . . you know, that awful newspaper piece . . .'

'What's so awful?' Lally asks, clearly anxious to keep the

subject away from her love life for as long as possible. 'I mean, since Emily doesn't want to carry on, it doesn't make much odds, does it?'

'I don't know.' Mum sighs. 'I don't know anything any more.' She fiddles with her napkin and glances across the table at me.

'I mean, quite apart from the wasted opportunity, what does it look like? All this stuff that reporter has written about the pressures of teenage tennis, competitive mothers, no social life? What does that make me look like?'

Lally cocks her head to one side and eyes Mum up and down.

'Oh – so the boot is on the other foot now!' she says, chuckling. 'Now perhaps you know how I felt when *you* were a teenager!'

To my surprise, Mum's neck turns a livid shade of red and she seems suddenly absorbed in picking invisible fluff off her skirt.

'Emily's not the only member of this family to hit the headlines, if you recall,' Lally says dryly. 'And at least she's not pictured in the company of two police officers, is she?'

'POLICE?' This is beginning to get interesting.

'Trust you to dig all that up!' Mum explodes. 'It wasn't my fault!'

'It never is,' Lally murmurs a little sarcastically.

'Well maybe,' Mum retorts, 'if you had managed to take your head out of your books for ten minutes and listened to what I wanted out of life, it wouldn't have happened.'

'What wouldn't have happened?' I cry. 'Will you tell me what you're talking about?'

'Nothing!' Mum mumbles.

'Oh come on, Ruth!' Lally protests. 'Seems to me this is truth time all round.' She turns to me. 'I messed up,' she says calmly. 'I admit that – I handled it all wrong. But the fact is your mother was one hell of a tearaway when she was sixteen and . . .'

'Mum? A tearaway?' She might as well try to convince me that my mother had taken holy orders.

'She got in with this ghastly, off the wall crowd of . . .'

'Oh for God's sake, Ma!' My mother pulls a face. 'If we are going to drag all that up again, you might as well tell it like it *really* was!'

She stomps over to the armchair, sits down and stares into space.

'So – what happened?' I urge her. 'How come you got arrested? What did –?'

'It happened in May of 1964,' Mum begins. 'I was exactly the same age as you are now – sixteen. And I'd just woken up to the fact that there was more to life than homework and O Levels. The whole country was swinging – that is, if you weren't a member of the Turnbull family living at 3 Lavender Gardens, Battersea.'

'That's not fair . . .' stammers Lally.

'Whose story is this?' demands my mother.

'Sorry,' replies Lally meekly. 'Carry on.'

'There was only one thing I was certain of back then,' Mum continues, 'and that was: no way was I going to end up like my parents. Dad was only interested in his four shops and his allotment – oh, and telling everyone how he'd gone up in the world, of course!'

Lally opened her mouth, caught Mum's eye and bit her lip.

'And you, Ma, were more clued up on the American Constitution than you were on what was going on under your own nose!'

She sounds fierce but I notice she smiles and pats Lally's hand.

'What I wanted was to *be* someone, to make a name for myself – and I knew exactly how I intended to do it!' She glances at me.

She must see the bewildered look on my face – my mother's life is hardly the stuff that makes a 'This is Your Life' programme.

'I wanted to go to art college,' she says with a touch of defiance.

'So? What was the problem?' I demand. It was hardly ground-breaking stuff, after all. Loads of people from my school do that every year.

'The problem,' declares my mother, 'was your grandmother. Ma just said I was going through a silly phase. She always said that when I suggested doing anything she didn't like.'

'Ruth, I . . .' Lally begins, but Mum ignores her and gabbles on.

'That spring, things really came to a head.' She sighed. 'I was fed up with being told what to do, what to wear, how to live my life. And yet I couldn't seem to find a way to make Ma listen to me.'

She half closes her eyes and leans back in her chair.

'We would go round and round in circles – me saying that art was all I was interested in, and Ma saying that people who permanently got A grades should be aiming for a "proper" career.

'For months, not one week went by without us arguing about it,' she recalls. 'And when Susie Timpson and her brother moved into the house opposite . . .'

Lally purses her lips and pulls a face.

'Oh, I know you never liked them!'

'Can you blame me? If you hadn't been so crazy about that awful boy and if Susie had had half a grain of common sense . . .'

'Lally, hush!' I hear myself say.

'Sorry.'

'The thing was,' Mum goes on, 'Susie was fun! OK, so she was a bit of a wild child – always getting detention, skipping school, that sort of thing – but she never did anything nasty or unkind. She and I became best friends – and Ma didn't like that one bit. I'll never forget the way she used to go on and on and on . . .'

RUTH

May 1964

'OUT OF ALL the girls at the High School, why do you have to pick that one to hang around with?' Ma looked up from the essay she was writing and glared at me.

'Because she's fun – F-U-N!' I retorted, sarcastically. 'Shall I get you the dictionary so you can look it up?'

'What's got into you these days?' Ma demanded, leaning back in her chair and fiddling with the bracelet on her left wrist. 'You used to be such a nice kid and now . . .'

'Now I'm not a kid any more – not that you'd notice!'

'Ruth!'

I realised I'd gone too far. I didn't usually dare speak to Mum like that, but I was desperate and, besides, Dad wasn't home. When he was around, it was more than my life was worth to raise my voice.

'OK, OK, I'm sorry – but Ma, everyone goes up to Carnaby Street on a Saturday – it's what you do!' I didn't add that Carnaby Street was only a tiny bit of what Susie and I had planned – I wasn't that stupid.

'Oh, it's not that I don't want you to have a good time, darling – it's just that you've got exams coming up . . .' my mother began, pushing her notepaper to one side and standing up.

'Exams, exams, exams!' I spat the words out. 'There is more to life, you know – and anyway, I'll work all day tomorrow.' I gave her a peck on the cheek. 'And Monday is a bank holiday so I can catch up then. I promise!'

I hopped from one leg to the other. Susie was leaving in ten minutes and I was afraid she wouldn't hang about if I wasn't ready.

'Well, you just make sure you do!' Ma insisted, pushing her papers to one side and opening an encyclopedia. 'If you don't get good grades in your O Levels, you won't be able to take the right Advanced Levels and then –'

'And then the sky will fall in!'

I knew I shouldn't be perpetuating the argument, and I knew I was being cheeky for the sake of it, but whenever Ma started on about schoolwork, I had this great urge to shake her. She knew quite well what I wanted to do – I'd been telling her every other day for three whole months – but I knew she would do all in her power to make sure it didn't happen.

'No, the sky won't fall in,' retorted Ma, 'but if you don't get to university, you'll end up like me – and according to you, that's the worst thing that could possibly happen!'

Too right! Apart from reading and helping out at the local orphanage a couple of mornings a week, all Ma ever did was housework and cooking. And even that was the same week in, week out – roast on Sunday, mince on Monday, fish pies on Friday.

'I like a routine,' she would tell me. 'That way, I know where I am and can get on with my studying.'

Ma was always learning something new – although personally, I couldn't see why she bothered. She read loads of books, spoke three languages, knew all about American history, and for what? It wasn't as if she had a job like some of my friends' mothers – although I was pretty certain she would have liked one. From time to time, I'd catch her looking at the job adverts in our local paper and once I even heard her mentioning a vacancy at the library to my father.

'Only two afternoons a week, Stanley, and I'd be home well in time to get you your tea,' she wheedled.

'I've said it before and I'll say it again,' Dad replied, in that slow, deliberate way of his, 'no wife of mine is going out to work. It's not right. It's up to the man to do the providing and the woman to keep the home nice.'

'Times change, Stan.'

'And not for the better!' Dad retorted and I knew just what was coming next – I'd heard it so often.

'I didn't fight in the war and lose a brother, just so that standards could drop and women . . .'

'You're right,' I heard Ma concede, and I wanted to shake her for giving in. 'Besides, I've plenty to do here.'

That's what always happened. Ma said we had to keep things calm for Dad because his nerves had been shot to pieces in the war and his health wasn't good. Personally, I thought he had just found a clever excuse for getting his own way all the time.

One thing was certain – Ma was right about me not wanting to end up like her. I was going to break free just as soon as I could – and I wasn't going to wait for A Levels and university to do it. Not that now was the moment to tell her.

'So I can go with Susie?' I asked.

Ma nodded. 'I suppose so,' she sighed, running her finger down the index at the back of her book. 'If you must. But no squandering all your birthday money on all that garish trash . . . oh, there it is! Battle of Little Big Horn. Now let me see . . .'

'Thanks, Ma!' I knew I'd won – once Ma's attention was caught by some boring battle, she'd be oblivious to anything else.

I was out into the hall in a flash and zipping up my white PVC boots. 'Won't be late!' I called.

'Oh, and take a coat!' she called after me. 'They're forecasting rain.'

And spoil the effect of my new white skinny rib jumper and red mini-skirt? I would rather have died of pneumonia.

❧

'You are still going to do it, aren't you?' Susie demanded as the Underground train clattered to a halt at Oxford Circus. 'You're not going to chicken out again?'

'Of course not!' I assured her. 'Look – I've even cut out the picture to make sure they do it right!' I shoved the crumpled cutting from *Queen* magazine into her hand.

'You do think it'll suit me, don't you?' I asked her,

fingering my shoulder-length hair nervously.

'You'll look stunning!' Susie assured me 'Now what do we do first – your hair or my photos?'

I stared at her. 'Photos? You mean – you really *are* going in for that competition? What does your mother think?'

'Mums?' She shrugged. 'Haven't the faintest idea – I haven't told her.'

I gasped.

That was one of the things that impressed – and amazed – me about Susie. She did her own thing all the time. When she came to the High School in the middle of the previous term, our teacher told me to look after Susie and help her get to know the ropes, as she put it. Some chance – Susie wasn't the least bit fazed by all the daft rules; she merely laughed at them and carried on regardless.

'Gals, skirts shall be two inches below the knee,' she would witter, mimicking Miss Ashwell, our stuffy headmistress, as she read from the list of regulations pinned outside the staff room door. 'Gals shall not run in corridors, slam doors or behave in a noisy or disorderly manner.'

Then she would turn to us. 'Gals in this place,' she'd declare 'will die of boredom!'

Everyone thought Susie was great, but to my astonishment, she picked *me* out as her number-one friend. I couldn't think why; we were as different as chalk from cheese. She was loud, I was timid; she was witty, I always thought of the punch line two hours too late. What's more, she was in the lowest stream for practically everything and I was – well, clever, I suppose. To be honest, there were times when I wished I was more like Susie. Having a 'good brain' was stopping me from doing the very thing I wanted most in the whole world.

'I can't believe you're actually going in for this Teenage Ambassador competition without your mum knowing,' I said as we hurried down Regent Street. 'What if you get a screen test?'

'What do you mean, "what if"? I *will* get a screen test.'

Confidence was another one of Susie's attributes. The moment she had seen that the *London Evening News* had got together with Columbia Pictures to find a teenager who would have the chance of a part in a Hollywood movie, she had been convinced it was meant for her.

'I'll tell my mother when she needs to know,' Susie assured me. 'Besides, you know my mum – she'll probably just nod vaguely and then forget who I am, never mind what I said to her!'

She had a point. Mrs Timpson was a sculptress. She spent her days in a converted summer house at the bottom of their garden, surrounded by wet clay and kilns. She wore long flowy skirts, smoked incessantly and let Susie and her brother Steve (who was utterly gorgeous) eat whatever they wanted and go out whenever the mood took them. I thought how wonderful it must be to have a mother who didn't ask questions, but just threw a five pound note at you and told you to enjoy yourself.

'I know!' Susie burst out, interrupting my reverie. 'We'll get your hair done first – then you can get photos taken with me!'

'What do I need photos for?' I asked.

'You have to have them when you apply to art college,' she said knowledgeably. 'I know because my cousin's at the Slade and she said . . .'

'I won't be applying to art college this year,' I replied sorrowfully. 'You know that – my parents haven't budged an inch!'

'So?' Susie stared at me in scorn. 'It's not them that want to be a world-famous fashion designer, is it? It's not their pictures that get scattered all through the school magazine, is it?'

'It's them that call the shots in my house!' I retorted. 'We don't all have parents like yours, you know.'

Susie grinned. 'Clearly,' she said, 'you haven't brought yours up properly. But it's never too late. You are going to art college and that's that!'

I knew she meant to encourage me; I knew I wanted it more than anything on earth. But I also knew that there was no way I could be like Susie and defy my parents.

'Says who?' I snapped.

'Says me!' she declared. 'And I always get what I want!'

I felt sick. My frizzy chestnut hair lay in little piles on the hair salon floor and I could feel the cold steel against the nape of my neck as the hairdresser put the finishing touches to my Kwan bob. I stared at the copy of *Pop Pics* in my lap, not daring to look at my reflection in the brightly lit mirror.

'How's that, madam?' My amusement at the title evaporated as I gingerly raised my eyes.

I looked amazing. My hair, sleek and shiny, was now chin length with a point caressing the bottom of each cheek. It was so sophisticated, so with it!

'It's smashing!' I couldn't hide my excitement. I didn't look like a schoolgirl any more; I looked like a woman, a real mod, someone to reckon with.

'Told you!' Susie beamed as we left the salon and headed off for the photo studio. 'You look like Mary Quant. Now all you have to do is get as famous as her!'

'If my mother doesn't kill me first,' I murmured.

But whether it was because of the new haircut, or simply because you couldn't be with Susie for long without some of her recklessness rubbing off on you, that Saturday was different from any other. We both had our photos taken – Susie in a dozen different starlet-style poses which she hoped would win her a Hollywood screen test in the competition and me trying to look mysterious and dynamic at the same time. The results in my case were rather ghost-like, enhanced by my mod make-up which Susie had insisted on applying in the ladies' loo at Liberty's.

'It's still not quite right,' she stated, surveying my black-rimmed eyes and deathly pale lips. 'I know – false eyelashes!'

I opened my mouth to protest and stopped. Why not? We ran to Carnaby Street, giggling all the way, and spent ten minutes in front of a mirror holding up ever longer lashes to our eyes. Within an hour I had the look; admittedly, I did have to keep my eyes wide open to stop the lashes sticking together but I didn't care.

'Stunning bone structure,' the photographer said, as he lined up his camera lens. 'And those eyes!'

OK, so he probably said the same thing to every woman that came through his door, but I soaked it up like a sponge.

'You're very lucky to have us here today,' Susie told him, fluttering her eyelashes and crossing her legs provocatively. 'When we're both famous, you'll be able to say it was your pictures that got us discovered!'

'Oh yes?' Somehow he didn't sound convinced.

'Yes,' Susie asserted. 'I'm going to be a film star and Ruth's going to be a top fashion designer. You'll see – five years from now, we'll be in all the glossies, isn't that right, Ruth?'

'Absolutely!'

And suddenly, in that moment, I started believing it. I knew I was good; I knew I could do it. It didn't matter that my mother and all my teachers said that art college was a waste of a good brain. I was my own person and no one would stop it.

'When can we have the pictures?' I asked.

'I'll post them off to you straight after the bank holiday,' the guy said. 'Better keep one back for myself – just in case you get famous!'

'Just in case? It's a dead cert!' said Susie, laughing.

'Right! Let's go!'

Susie grabbed my arm and dragged me towards the Underground station.

'Hang on!' I protested. 'We haven't done the shops yet!'

'Later!' Susie insisted. 'There's somewhere you have to go.'

'Where? What's going on?'

Susie sighed. 'Just for once,' she pleaded, 'trust me. It's all for your own good.'

I pulled a face.

'That's parent-speak for it's horrible, boring and a waste of time!'

Susie grinned. 'Oh, this isn't a waste of time!' she said. 'This is the day you start to fulfil your destiny!'

'Susie, we can't just walk in!'

I stopped dead in my tracks, staring up at the ugly grey building ahead of me, with its vast sign above the door – Thameside College of Art and Design.

'Of course we can, silly!' Susie was beginning to sound exasperated. 'It's an art college, for heaven's sake, not the Houses of Parliament!' She grabbed my hand and dragged me up the steps and through the glass doors.

'This is fab!'

The buzz hit me the moment we got inside. The foyer was surrounded by studios, their doors flung open to reveal a hive of creative activity. Some students were painting, others building wire sculpture, yet more making what looked like a collage out of dry bones and old paper bags. And everywhere there was the wonderful smell of oil paints, turpentine and wet clay.

'I knew you'd love it – Mums came here and she says it's divine,' Susie enthused.

Of course I knew all about Thameside. Not only did it have a reputation for producing some of the country's top modern artists and sculptors but also the students were always in the news. They had staged sit-ins against apartheid in South Africa, chanted American civil rights songs on the college steps, and marched along the Embankment waving banners and shouting anti-nuclear slogans. A few of the students had been arrested for lying prone in the middle of the road during the rush hour and bringing traffic to a standstill.

'They should never have done away with National Service,' my dad grumbled every time the news covered one of the stories. 'The whole country is going to pot – we're raising a nation of self-centred young louts!'

'Dad, if they were self-centred, they wouldn't be fighting for other people's rights!' I kept telling him.

But the reply was always the same. 'You don't know the half of it, young lady! You didn't fight in the war and . . .'

And so it went on. And on and on.

One thing was certain, my father was hardly going to jump at the idea of his only daughter going to Thameside.

'Come on!' Susie broke into my thoughts, grabbing my hand and dragging me up to a desk marked 'Enquiries'.

'Can I help?' The receptionist smiled at us.

'Yes,' declared Susie before I could open my mouth. 'We'd like to see someone about Admissions, please. I did say we'd be coming.'

'You . . .' I was speechless.

'Up the stairs, third door on the right. You'll find everything you need up there.'

I waited until we were out of earshot before laying into Susie.

'We can't do this!' I protested. 'I mean – I'm not prepared and I haven't brought any pictures and . . .'

'I have!' Susie snapped open her bag and pulled out a couple of small sheets of paper. 'I nicked these from the Art Room display.' She waved them in my face.

'I know they're tiny,' she sighed, 'but none of the bigger ones would have fitted into my bag.'

I stared at the pictures, one a design for a wedding dress, the other a portrait of an old lady, and suddenly I felt like bursting into tears.

'You've done all this . . . just because I want to get to art college?'

''Course!' Susie chirped, striding up the stairs two at a time. 'After all, when I'm a Hollywood legend, I have to have someone to design my dresses, don't I? I can see it now: *Susie Sheen wore a glittering gown by the coveted designer, Ruth Less*.'

I giggled despite my nervousness. 'Susie *Sheen*? *Ruth Less*? You're crazy!'

'Whatever!' She laughed. 'We have to change our names – you can't be famous with surnames like Timpson and Turnbull, can you?'

'Timpson and Turnbull!' I breathed, stopping dead in my tracks. 'That's what I'll call it.'

'Call what?'

'My boutique,' I said. 'No – The Two Tees! How's that for a label?'

'Like it!'

Susie gave me a quick hug and pushed open the door marked 'Course Information – Apply Within'.

'We've come about art courses,' she began. 'This is Ruth Turnbull and she's amazing. Look!'

She shoved my two pictures at the astonished tutor.

'Now – when can she start?'

'I can't believe it!' I said for the tenth time as the tube rattled its way back to Oxford Circus. 'Have you seen this?' I flicked to another page in the glossy prospectus. 'And this?'

'Ruth, you've shown me every paragraph a dozen times!' Susie sighed. 'I could recite the wretched thing to you!'

'Do you think this will be enough to convince Ma?' I asked. 'At least enough to let me apply?'

'Sure to,' Susie reassured me, as the train pulled into the station. 'Now *please* could we forget about Foundation Courses and Abstract Design and go shopping?'

Three hours, two frothy coffees and a shared banana split later, we headed for home. I caught sight of my reflection in a shop window and couldn't believe my eyes. My new Lennon cap perched on top of my freshly bobbed hair was stunningly set off by the huge button earrings Susie had persuaded me to buy.

But they were nothing compared to my prize purchase

– a bright orange and purple mini-dress, the shortest I'd ever had. It looked so good with my long white boots that I couldn't resist keeping it on once I'd paid for it. And I got so many wolf-whistles from boys in Carnaby Street that even Susie began to look jealous.

'So you know what you've got to do?' she demanded on the train on the way home.

'Show the prospectus to Ma, tell her that the future lies in fashion and design and . . .' I hesitated.

'. . . and that they may as well agree because you'll do it anyway!' finished Susie triumphantly.

I knew quite well that I could never in a million years speak to my mother like that, but I simply nodded.

'That's that then!' declared Susie. 'Now – what shall we wear on Monday?'

'Monday? What's happening on Monday?'

'Oh, didn't I say? We're going to Brighton. You, me, this gorgeous new guy I met at the coffee bar last week . . .'

'I can't,' I began. 'My mother would never let me and . . .'

'Steve's going! And he asked if you'd be there!'

Steve? Susie's adorable, gorgeous, sexy brother? Actually wanting me to go on a day out?

'Live a little, Ruth,' Susie urged. 'Practise for freedom!'

I grinned. 'Actually,' I said, 'Brighton would be fab. Just fab.'

I walked up the path to my house on cloud nine. I felt sophisticated, sexy, as if I could conquer the world.

The feeling lasted precisely three minutes.

'Your hair! What have you done to your hair?' My father was standing in the hallway staring at me.

'Had it cut,' I replied boldly even though my heart was thumping. 'Do you like . . . ?'

'And what have you got plastered all over your face? And that dress – showing all that thigh – it's disgraceful!'

'It's the fashion, Dad,' I began.

'Not in this house, it's not!' he retorted. 'Alice!'

He yelled towards the kitchen, from which Ma emerged wiping her hands on a drying-up cloth.

'Oh, Ruth!' she gasped.

'Get upstairs now – and clean yourself up!' Dad commanded.

I didn't dare argue; there was too much at stake. I bit my tongue and meekly trotted upstairs, changed into jeans, washed my face and then spent the next hour being nauseatingly good, peeling potatoes, laying the table and generally sucking up to Ma and Dad.

'The hair's not too bad, actually,' Ma whispered, furiously mashing up potato. 'Better than the dress, at any rate.'

She turned to me with a slight smile. 'Don't mind your dad,' she said. 'He'll get used to it – you know what he's like.'

I knew all right, but Ma's words gave me the courage to push the boundaries a bit further.

'I've got something to show you,' I began tentatively to Ma and Dad during supper. 'Something I brought back from London.'

'Not more trash, I hope,' muttered my mother, her generous moment clearly having passed.

'No – this!' I shoved the prospectus into her hand. 'Oh Ma, it's amazing – you've never seen anywhere like it.'

'But this is Thameside College!' my mother exclaimed.

I took a deep breath, determined not to go on the defensive.

'That's right!' I continued eagerly. 'There's all these different courses; you start with an Art Foundation course for a year and then you choose . . .'

'Wait!' My mother held up a hand. 'Before you go any further – you are not seriously suggesting that you attend this . . . this place?' She slapped the brochure on to the dining table as if it were contaminated with bubonic plague.

'Yes, I am!' I snatched it up again and thrust it at Dad. 'It's got an amazing reputation . . .'

'It has a reputation,' my father said, in his slow, laboured way, 'as a hotbed of student politics! I've seen it on the television – sit-ins, marches, chanting youths . . .'

'But Dad, students do that kind of thing, it doesn't mean . . .'

'It means they have no regard, no respect, for what we fought for in the war!' Dad declared, thumping the table.

'Don't upset yourself, Stanley!' Ma murmured, just the way she always did. I was incandescent. Once again, Dad was using the war as an excuse not to talk about anything new or modern or exciting.

'Thameside's one of the best colleges there is!' I cried. 'Susie's mum went there and . . .'

'Well, that says it all, doesn't it?' Ma intervened, glancing anxiously at Dad's ever-reddening face. 'Darling, I know you think we're being mean but we're saying all this for your own good . . .'

'That's what you always say!' I cried, pushing back my chair and jumping to my feet. 'You don't mean it though – you're saying it for YOUR good. To stop me doing what I want, to keep me under your thumb forever. Well, it won't work! I'm going to art college, whether you like it or not.'

'I can't take this . . .' My father staggered to his feet, his face puce and his hand trembling.

'Now look what you've done!' my mother hissed 'How dare you upset your father? We say these things because we have more experience of life than you do and . . .'

'Oh yes? And what do you really know? Dad's stuck in a shop all day and you're stuck around the house. You wouldn't even know there was a world out there!'

'I've had enough of this!' my father declared. 'Go to your room.'

'Wait, Stanley!' Ma stood up and took my hand.

'Listen, darling,' she said, swallowing hard. 'You have a wonderful brain – you're great at languages and your History reports are always excellent. It would be such a waste to go to some art college when you could go to university and be a teacher or –'

'I don't want to be a teacher!' I wailed. 'I want to be a fashion designer. Or maybe an interior designer or . . .'

'There you are, you see – you don't even know your

own mind! Ruth, it's a phase . . .'

That did it. That stupid word again. I'd had enough.

'You just don't care about what I want, do you?' I spluttered. 'I wish I had normal parents instead of a couple of old-fashioned, boring, unambitious . . .' I ran out of words, partly because I was sobbing too much to think straight and partly because the only one that came to mind would certainly have had me grounded for eternity.

'I've told you to go to your room!' my father thundered.

'Gladly!' I choked. 'But I'll never change my mind! Never!'

I think I might have calmed down, might have been prepared to listen to them just one more time, if it hadn't been for what they did that evening while I was in my room. They threw the Thameside prospectus in the dustbin.

It was like a slap in the face – as if my dreams, my hopes, meant no more to them than a load of rotting garbage. I hunted through the bin and I found it – wet, smelly and stained. The application form had been torn into pieces.

'The subject is closed, Ruth,' Ma said sternly as I began protesting yet again. 'You'll thank us in the end, you know – once you're at university having a great time and getting the tools for a proper career.'

She paused.

'I would have given anything to have the opportunities you have,' she said softly. 'But what with my father being killed and my mother dying . . .'

Her voice trailed off and suddenly I felt deflated. Deflated and guilty. After all, I'd heard the story of her life a dozen times and each time I was almost moved to tears by it. The thought of her mother being blown up in the street, clutching the coin meant for Ma's pocket money was so poignant. I couldn't imagine how I'd feel if I were left alone with no parents.

'Your father means well,' she went on. 'You know his nerves won't take arguments; but he loves you, and that's why he knows that all this art nonsense is out of the question. The way to be safe in this world is to have a job that lasts you a lifetime, a job in which people respect you . . .'

I didn't reply. I hadn't the energy.

'Can I go and see Susie?' I asked flatly.

'Of course you can!' Ma was clearly so relieved that I'd changed the subject that even Susie's supposed shortcomings could be overlooked.

'I love you, Ruth!' she called after me.

I pretended not to hear. I was determined not to make life too easy for her. After all, she was still set on ruining mine.

'Hey! You look as if you could happily murder someone!'

As I stomped up the path to Susie's front door, her brother Steve came careering out of the garage, revving the engine of his Lambretta.

'If it wasn't illegal, I probably would!' Actually, I was quite proud of myself for the quick retort – usually just seeing Steve Timpson would reduce me to pulp.

'It's the illegal things that are the most fun!' he teased. 'Want to come for a spin?' I stared at him.

'What, me? Now?'

'Yeah. Why not? Have you got something better to do?'

'I was going to see Susie but . . . I'd love to come!' I swung my leg over the moped and wrapped my arms around his waist.

'Hang on, kid!' he shouted above the revving engine. I turned to look at my house, praying that my mother would see me going off with Steve. That would show her, prove that she couldn't rule every corner of my life.

But there was no sign of anyone at the window.

Steve revved once more and sped off down the road.

Heaven had actually come to Lavender Gardens.

'You're a dark horse!' Susie teased an hour later when Steve and I returned, windswept and flushed. 'Practising for Monday, were you?'

I knew that if I went off to the coast with them I'd be in awful trouble at home but what else was new? At least I'd be having fun.

'Seven o'clock tomorrow morning, then!' Steve announced, patting the seat of his Lambretta. 'We want as much time at Brighton as we can get.'

'We're going all the way to Brighton on that?' I gasped.

'Do you have a problem with that?'

'No, of course not,' I gabbled. 'It'll be a lark.'

And to start with, it was.

‘There’s hundreds of them – where have they all come from?’

The road to Brighton was awash with mods on Vespas and Lambrettas, buzzing along like hyperactive bumblebees. Car drivers tooted their horns in irritation as some of the braver ones weaved their way in front of them, often making none too polite gestures as they did.

‘This is nothing!’ Steve shouted back at me. ‘You wait till we get there – last Easter there were loads of us. And rocker scum as well, of course! Did *we* let rip!’

For the first time, a shiver of unease rippled through my body, but I told myself I was simply cold. I was wearing my new mini-dress and a cardigan, but they didn’t seem to be keeping me warm, despite the May sunshine. The journey from Battersea seemed to take for ever and my bottom was numb.

‘Isn’t this the best thing?’ Susie shouted as she and her new boyfriend, Bry, pulled up level with us. ‘And this weather should bring them all out!’

‘All *who*?’ I yelled, but they had nipped past us and my words were lost on the wind.

I still couldn’t believe my own daring. The day before, Ma had said the Brighton trip was out of the question.

‘You know we always go to Box Hill for a picnic on Whit Monday,’ she protested.

‘Precisely!’ I had shouted back. ‘And for once, I’m going to do something different.’

Of course, she told me I was selfish, said that girls my age should spend time with their families, not with a load of tearaways.

'Do you understand?' she had demanded.

I had nodded. I understood only too well. If I wanted a life, there was only one thing to do – rebel.

The note I had shoved under Ma and Dad's door while they slept that morning simply read '*Gone to Brighton; don't worry. Back tonight. Love Roo*'.

But despite my bravado, my stomach was doing acrobatics. I could just imagine their reaction when they found the note – and the row there would be when I got home.

But there was one thing they couldn't do: they couldn't take the fun I was having from me. It would be too late.

It was when we reached the outskirts of Brighton things began to hot up. Just as we reached the junction of the London and Lewes roads, a dozen boys on 500 Norton motorbikes roared out from a side street and raged past us, shouting and swearing.

'Rockers!' proclaimed Steve, sounding exhilarated. I clung on to his waist even tighter as he swung his Lambretta into the kerb.

'They scared me!' I admitted, and then, catching the fleeting look of scorn on Steve's face, I realised my mistake. 'Only joking!'

We parked up by the West Pier alongside scores of mods. I had thought I looked the part when we'd left home, but now I just felt like a schoolkid playing at dressing up. I didn't have a suede coat, I didn't even have Hush Puppies like Susie – and worst of all, I didn't know the routine.

'First we go to El Espresso for a coffee,' Susie said, slipping her arm through mine and heading up East Street.

'And anything else that's going,' added Steve with a chuckle.

I was starving and the thought of getting a cream cake or even a wagon wheel added a spring to my step.

The café was buzzing. The jukebox was blaring out the latest Supremes hit, 'Baby Love', and everyone was bopping and singing along. But there were no cream cakes to be seen.

Steve and Bry disappeared into a corner with a load of other boys while Susie and I sipped our coffees and plied the jukebox with shillings. Other girls came up and chatted to us and I felt for the first time in my life as if I was part of the real scene.

'I wish I'd brought my sketch pad,' I told Susie. 'I want to get it all down on paper!'

'Here!' She pulled open her clutch bag and shoved a tiny notebook into my hand. 'It's not much, but it's a start.'

'OK, chicks, let's hit the beaches!' Steve called out a few minutes later, interrupting my sketching and dragging us from our seats.

After that things happened really fast. We piled across the road and leaned over the railings, and at once I could see that this was no ordinary sunbathing, swimming crowd. Large groups of rockers were sitting on the breakwaters and pacing up and down the shoreline, while other, smaller groups of mods leaned over the railings on the promenade and shouted things at them.

'I can feel the buzz, man!' Steve said suddenly, turning to Bry. 'What d'ya think?'

'Let's show them!'

And they were gone, vaulting the railings, crashing down on to the pebbles below and running full pelt towards the nearest group of rockers. It was as if a secret signal had been fired. Within seconds the beach was a mass of running, shouting boys.

'Oh, Ruth, stop him!' Susie grabbed my arm and stared open mouthed at her brother. 'He's had some stuff, I know he has!'

'Stuff?'

'Don't you know anything?' Fear was making her angry. 'Purple Hearts, stupid – he got them at the café, I'm sure of it.'

'He wouldn't be that stupid!' I protested. 'He's just . . .'

I was interrupted by a piercing scream and then a deck-chair flew through the air.

'Bry, Steve, no!' In a flash, Susie was gone, rushing down the steps and across the stones, stumbling in her haste. Bry and Steve and a few other mods were belting across the beach, shouting and knocking over deck-chairs as they went.

I felt as if my feet were glued to the pavement. I couldn't believe what was happening. As I stood there more motorbikes roared up, and another gang of rockers careered on to the beach, shortly followed by a crowd of mods, some wielding cricket bats, others picking up stones and hurling them. Mums and dads with small kids were fleeing the beach in panic, spilling picnic baskets and rubber rings behind them.

And then I spotted Susie. She was standing on the edge of a crowd of guys who were brawling.

Or at least she was for a moment. Within a second, she was in the midst of it, punching her fists into the back of a leather-jacketed rocker.

I honestly can't remember running across the shingle. I have no idea how I got there so fast.

'Leave him alone!' Susie screamed, grabbing the guy's arm. She didn't stand a chance. He simply sneered, wrenched his arm away and she went flying.

That's when I saw Steve and Bry. They were in the middle of the group, surrounded by rockers – girls as well as boys – and so outnumbered that they didn't stand a chance either. Steve's lip was bleeding and Bry was in an armlock, caught between two broad-shouldered boys with studded leather jackets.

'Get the others!' Susie stammered, clambering to her feet. 'That lot over there!'

She gestured to a crowd of mods who were bounding across the beach overturning deck-chairs. As I was following her gaze, I saw police cars screeching to a halt on the promenade, and dozens of uniformed constables jumping out and heading our way.

'Susie, we've got to get out of here!' I implored her.

'It's getting nasty and . . .'

'. . . and you're chickening out, is that it?' she shouted back. 'That's my brother in the middle of all that – the one who's supposed to be your boyfriend!'

The words hit me like a thunderbolt. I mean, Steve was gorgeous and fun, and . . . my boyfriend? Part of me was thrilled. He must have told Susie that he fancied me; she certainly didn't get the idea from me. But part of me wished she hadn't said it. To be honest, I wasn't sure that I wanted a boyfriend who got caught up in fights.

But then something happened that put paid to all my musings. A stone flew through the air and hit Susie squarely on the lips. The blood trickled down her chin and on to her white polo-neck.

I forgot Steve and I forgot the police. I wheeled around and came face-to-face with a sneering, greasy-haired rocker who, for all his swagger, wasn't much taller than I was.

'Was that you?' I snarled. 'Because if it was . . .'

And I punched him.

It's easy to say I was stupid. It's easy to say that I should never have interfered in the first place. But Susie was my friend and, besides, I reckon all the bottled-up anger from the previous few days just spilled over into that one reckless moment.

How reckless, I was about to find out.

The guy roared with laughter. 'Oooh! Who tapped me?' he jeered.

I shoved him away. 'Pig!' I shouted.

'That'll do!' A firm hand grabbed me and pulled me

back. 'You just come with me, missy!'

'She didn't do anything!' Susie protested, snatching at the constable's sleeve. 'Leave her alone, you bully!' Which meant, of course, that she got arrested too.

As we were being marched up the steps and on to the promenade, cameras started flashing. I'm quite sure that dozens of pictures were taken. I guess the sight of two kids being frog-marched towards a police car crying and struggling was something of a novelty.

They didn't charge us. They kept us at the police station for a couple of hours and then sent us packing.

Bry and Steve weren't so lucky. They were charged with causing an affray. I heard they might have been let off, but Steve got really lippy with the police officer and that put paid to any idea of leniency. Luckily we had just enough cash between us to pay for the rail fare home.

It was only lunch time, and the day was ruined.

'I never knew your brother was like that,' I said to Susie as we plodded up Queen's Road to the railway station.

'Like what?' Susie was immediately on the defensive.

'Well . . . aggressive,' I ventured.

'He's not,' she retaliated. But then her tone grew softer. 'Well, he wasn't – not until he started popping Purple Hearts.'

I couldn't believe my ears.

'I kept telling him he was stupid,' she said. 'But he's doing A Levels – he said he used them to stay awake, and I sort of thought that it would be OK, just for a while, you know.'

She sighed. 'I never realised that they would make him so . . . well, speeded up.'

'What on earth is your mother going to say?' I asked.

Susie looked at me as if I had taken leave of my senses.

'Say? She's not going to say anything because we're not going to tell her.'

'But even if you don't tell her about the pills, she's bound to want to know where Steve is!'

Susie shrugged. 'I'll say he met up with some mates and decided to stay over with them,' she muttered. 'And don't you dare tell the truth, OK?'

'And what about your lip?'

The bleeding had stopped but Susie's mouth was bruised and swollen.

'I fell off the Lambretta,' she stressed. 'Got it? Not a *word* about what really happened.'

We didn't talk much on the way home. The nearer the train got to Battersea, the more nervous I felt. I knew the sort of trouble I would be in – and really, it hadn't been worth it.

'Let's go for a walk,' Susie suggested. 'If we get back too early, the oldies are bound to smell a rat.'

She had a point. We spent the next two hours wandering round the park, drinking coffees we didn't really want, and trying to pretend that everything would be fine, really.

That morning I'd felt as if I could conquer the world and now I felt grubby, tired and fed up.

'I will never, ever trust you again!' My mother stood in the hallway, her face so pale that it seemed transparent, her hands clenching and unclenching as she barred my way.

'What you have done to this family . . . !' Her voice trailed off and she began to cry.

'Ma, I only went out for the day! It's not a crime!'

'Oh really?' My mother grabbed me by the arm and forced me into the kitchen. 'So what do you call that?' She stabbed a finger at the *Evening Standard*, lying on the table.

I gasped. The newspaper swam before my eyes. In that moment, all the carefully rehearsed excuses evaporated into thin air. There, on the front page in stark black and white, was a photograph of Susie, me and two policemen.

And we weren't just having a friendly chat.

'*It's not just boys causing mayhem on the beaches*,' read the caption. '*Girls can be tearaways too*.'

'I never thought,' choked Ma, 'that a daughter of mine would be . . .'

'Ma, listen!' I pleaded, suddenly regaining my composure. 'It's not what it seems – Susie's brother was . . .'

'I am *not* interested!' she shouted. 'First, you defy your father and me by going out when we strictly forbade it, and then you get yourself blazoned across the newspapers for all to see! You are despicable!'

'Does Dad . . . ?'

'Your father is lying down,' she spat. 'He phoned the police station in Brighton. It's a wonder the shock didn't kill him. You know he can't take upsets, not after what happened in the –'

'The war – I know!' I didn't mean to sound sarcastic but the words were out before I could stop them.

'You don't have the first idea, do you?' Ma retaliated. 'The sacrifices I've made – we've made – for you . . . and *this* is how you repay us!'

It went on for days. Dad hardly spoke to me; Ma checked up on me every five minutes. Susie was great. She tried to tell Ma it was all her fault and that I'd only been trying to help her and her brother, but Ma was really rude and just told her that she wasn't welcome in the house.

I hated her for that.

And then we had parents' evening at school.

It was all cut and dried before we even got to see the headmistress. If I'd had any sense, I would have realised that.

'Under normal circumstances,' Miss Ashwell intoned, 'such behaviour as was displayed by Ruth last week would have resulted in instant expulsion.'

She paused for the weight of her words to be fully absorbed.

'But,' she went on, 'following our little chats . . .' She beamed at my mother. '. . . we will accept Ruth into the Sixth Form. She has a good brain; she could go far.'

'I don't want . . .' I began.

'I rather think,' stressed Miss Ashwell, 'that what you do or do not want at this point in time is rather beside the point, don't you? You have hardly shown yourself mature enough to make rational decisions.'

She sniffed and hitched her bosom into a more comfortable position.

'Art colleges are for those who lack the academic potential to go further,' she said. 'You are university material. I am relying on you to repay your parents by working hard and making something of yourself.'

And that was that.

❧

I found the picture years later – the one I'd scribbled on Susie's notepad in the coffee bar that morning in Brighton.

It was good.

No, it was brilliant. It had movement, it captured the atmosphere; you could almost feel the buzz.

There was no point keeping it. It belonged to the past.

After all, what did a twenty-five-year-old History teacher want with a pencil drawing of what might have been?

EMILY

June

'I DON'T GET IT!'

All through Mum's story, my frustration has been building and now I feel as if I could explode.

'What?' Mum looks genuinely puzzled.

'You are such a hypocrite!' Even Lally looks aghast as I thump the table. 'You've been going on about how Lally stopped you doing what you really wanted – and now you're doing exactly the same thing to me!'

Mum shakes her head vehemently. 'No, darling – can't you see? I'm doing the exact opposite!'

'Oh, please!'

Mum touches my hand tentatively. 'I'm trying to avoid you making the same mistakes I made!' she persists. 'Settling for some boring career when you could be hitting the headlines, making a name for yourself, earning good money . . .' Her voice faltered.

'You know what happened to me in 1998,' she reminded me.

I swallowed hard. Mum had been ill and the doctor said it was all due to stress in the classroom. She used to teach in a huge comprehensive on the edge of Brighton – one of the real sink schools – and in the end it all got to be too much. She used to cry all the time and have nightmares, and her skin broke out in this awful rash. She had to give up her job and couldn't work for ages.

'I don't want you to end up the same way,' Mum sighs. 'This silly idea about risking your life in some Godforsaken part of the world . . .'

'There you go again!' I shout. 'It's not a silly idea and besides, it's not Godforsaken – it's where God wants me to –'

'That church has brainwashed you!' Mum jumps to her feet and then just as suddenly slumps back in the chair. 'Can't you see? Supposing you get married and the guy does a runner, just like your wretched father?'

Here we go again. My memory of Dad gets fainter by the year, but I still hate it when she slags him off like that. Not that he doesn't deserve it – he left us when I was six. He went to Argentina with some woman from his office and promised that when I was old enough, he'd invite me out for holidays but he never did. Nowadays he sends a cheque once a year on my birthday.

I never cash it.

But I'm not seeing what this has to do with what I choose to do with my life.

'Get in with a man like your father and you'd have to earn money to keep body and soul together! And believe me, dishing up rice to a load of refugees isn't the way to do it!'

'Mum!'

She bites her lip. To be fair, she looks pretty embarrassed.

Her neck turns red and she starts drumming her fingers on the table.

'OK, I'm sorry – maybe that was a bit over the top,' she concedes. 'I suppose there's no point arguing with you. You know it all, and clearly my opinions count for nothing.'

'It's not like that . . .' I begin, but she stops me with a wave of her hand.

'I'm sorry, Emily.' She throws her arms round me and hugs me. 'I don't know what to think . . . I just want what's best for you. It's a dog-eat-dog world out there, darling.'

I see my chance in an instant. 'Well, if I take my A Levels, I'll be able to get a good job, even if I change my mind about charity work,' I say quickly. I'm pretty sure I won't change my mind, but I can tell that my remark has hit home.

'That's true . . .' she begins. Lally is on her feet.

'Absolutely!' Lally cries. 'So that's all settled then.'

'Settled for you, Ma,' Mum mutters. 'And settled for Emily. But what about me?'

'You?' Lally and I speak in unison.

'Yes, me!' Mum cries. 'Not that I imagine either of you have given me a thought!'

'What is it, dear?' asks Lally calmly. 'I can't see how all this is going to affect your plans . . .'

'Oh, can't you? If we're not all living here, I can't build a business, can I? You said I could use the conservatory as a studio. I had plans – I was going to advertise, make something of my mural painting – do what I wanted for the first time in my life!'

The words tumble out so quickly that I can hardly grasp what she is saying.

'And there's no reason why you shouldn't do that!' Lally insists.

'Oh sure!' Mum retorts. 'If you're not here, helping with the bills, seeing to Emily if I'm away . . .' Her voice falters.

'Ruth dear, just calm down,' orders Lally. 'The money you would have spent on Emily's coaching can go towards building your business. She'll get a grant for university and she can spend her long vacations with me in Montana.'

Hang on.

'What?' Mum and I speak as one.

'Well,' Lally says, looking a little sheepish, 'I shall miss her. Both of you. Assuming I get there . . .'

'Why wouldn't you?' I ask, half hoping the plan might be falling through already.

She sighs and looks at her bare wrist. 'I know it's ridiculous,' she says, and her eyes are moist, 'but we had this pact, Zack and I. He said I was to wear the bracelet until the day he made me his own – and then he'd buy me a ring. And the bracelet is . . .' Her voice cracks. '. . . gone!'

I never realised old people could have all these romantic ideas in their head.

'It'll turn up,' Mum says weakly.

'Maybe.' I can tell Lally doesn't believe it. 'Anyway, as I was saying, Emily can spend her vacations with me in the States – she could even play in some tournaments, just to keep her hand in, and that way you'd both be happy.'

'No, Lally!' I'm surprised how steady my voice is. 'I'd

love to come and visit you for a week or two, but that's all. I'm not leaving Mum all on her own.'

I smile tentatively at my mother. She looks really small and bewildered.

'Besides, I'll be getting holiday jobs in care homes and stuff like that,' I tell them. 'Stuff that will look good on my CV. From now on, tennis is a hobby. Nothing more.'

For a long time, Mum says nothing. Then, with a long, deep sigh, she stands up.

'Right,' she says, surprisingly calm. 'From now on, then, I'll just concentrate on me, shall I? Since everyone else is doing their own thing, I might as well join you.'

We don't say any more. We just get up and start clearing the table and Mum starts nagging about the time and unfinished homework and the fact that I still haven't ironed my PE kit.

It's about as normal as we've been for ages.

As if.

We get home from Lally's to find the answer phone flashing like a thing demented.

'*Get Emily to telephone me first thing tomorrow morning – I have things to say to her!*' That one from Felix.

'*Happy to say we have an offer on your house at the full asking price!*' That from the estate agents.

'*Emily – tried your mobile loads of times but it was switched off. Are you avoiding me? It's not like it seems. You have to phone. Please!*' That, and another five like it, from Hugo.

'How that boy has the audacity!' my mother explodes,

and I'm inclined to agree with her.

'Don't worry,' I tell her. 'I'll call him tomorrow and tell him where to go!'

'It's good to see you have some sense in one area of your life!' Mum replies. 'Pity it doesn't extend to everything you do.'

Some parents can't let it go. I take this as a cue to go upstairs.

I manage to hold off for all of five minutes before I'm on the phone to Hugo.

'So that's what you call trust!' I begin before he can utter a word. 'You promised it wouldn't go into the paper! I bet there isn't any competition – you lied to me . . .'

'Emily, will you just shut up and let me –'

'*Don't* you tell me to shut up!' I storm. 'You got me into the most awful trouble with my mother, you broke a confidence, you –'

'*I* didn't do anything!' he shouts. 'I showed my piece to the editor to get his signature on the entry form and he whisked it away and said he wanted it in the paper today!'

I'm gripping the phone in my fury.

'Oh, and I suppose you just let him!' I spit the words. 'You could have said no – or doesn't your vocabulary stretch that far?'

'I tried!' His voice has taken on a pleading tone. 'But he wasn't having any of it – said that it was a great piece of reportage – he even gave me a byline!'

He can't disguise the note of pride in his voice but I'm not interested.

'I don't care if he gave you a one-way ticket to Fiji!' I shout. 'It would serve you right if I sued you!'

'Oh do what you like!' he retorts. 'Pity I didn't put in a paragraph about a spoiled brat who thinks only of herself!'

'How dare you . . .' I begin. But the phone goes dead.

I was so furious that I thought I'd be awake all night, but the next thing I know the alarm is shrilling in my ear and my mother is hammering on the door.

'Felix is on the phone!' she hisses. 'He wants to speak to you.'

My heart starts pounding.

'Can't you say I'm . . . ?' I begin.

'No way!' my mother says. 'It's your mess.'

I wrench open the door and thunder down the stairs.

'Emily, wait!' Mum calls. 'You . . . I mean, you *are* sure you're doing the right thing? It's not too late to change your mind.'

Stupidly, I hesitate. The thing is, I mean – what if I *am* wrong? What if I flunk my A Levels? What if no university wants me and I've given up tennis and all I'm stuck with is some boring job?

'Talk it over with Felix,' my mother pleads. 'I'm convinced it's just nerves, darling – you're feeling daunted by the thought of . . .'

That snaps me back. There she goes again, presuming that she knows my every thought.

'I'm certain, Mum,' I tell her, grabbing the handset. 'Absolutely certain.'

Felix holds forth for ages about my rampant disobedience in talking to the press, my foolhardiness in leaping off walls when I have my ankles and wrists to consider, and my obvious penchant for alcohol and wild living.

'Felix, there's something you . . .' I begin but he's off again and in the end I just sit here at the bottom of the stairs and let him rant on.

But eventually, just as he's about to ring off, I tell him I'm quitting.

He thinks I'm a spoiled brat. He says that I'm letting my country down by refusing to develop my 'God-given talent' and bring British tennis back to the forefront of world sport.

'You should be listening to your mother,' he rages. 'She's sacrificed a whole heap of stuff for you.'

As if I didn't know that. As if I didn't feel guilty enough already. Suddenly I feel all too aware that this is the moment that changes everything. I feel panic overtaking me. *Am* I being childish? Do I know what I'm doing?

I suppose I could give it a go, and then if it doesn't work out, I could do A Levels later and . . .

'And think of the money you could make!' Felix goes on. 'We're talking mega bucks here, kiddo, if you give it your all.'

I could buy Mum all the things she's never had. I could have a flat of my own. And a car . . .

'OK, so maybe I was a bit over the top just now,' he admits. 'I know that once your training has started, you'll put all this partying behind you and focus on the one thing that matters. Tennis.'

I swallow hard, my resolve back in full force.

'Felix, I'm really grateful and I'm honoured that you think me worth wasting time over,' I begin. There are times when grovelling has its place.

'I know, kid,' he says, and you can hear the relief in his voice. 'We'll just say no more about it and . . .'

'No, wait!' I'm amazed at my boldness. 'You see, I know that if I take up the scholarship, I owe it to everyone to push everything else out of my life.' I take a deep breath. 'And I can't. There are things that matter more to me.'

The silence goes on for so long that I think he has hung up, but suddenly he coughs.

'And what are these *things*?' He sounds as if he expects me to list street drugs, mad orgies and lavish spending.

'I want to work for a charity. Abroad. With refugees. Make a difference.' The words don't come out as I mean them to.

'But honey, that's OK! In fact, that's wonderful!' Felix enthuses.

He understands! I can't believe it.

'The press love that kind of stuff – you know, *Tennis star mopping brow of fevered child*.'

I don't believe I'm hearing this.

'Look at it this way! If you get to the top in tennis – and with me behind you, it's a dead cert! – you can write as many cheques for as many charities as you want. No problem!'

I owe this guy a big favour. Because in that second, as he spoke, I knew. I knew why I wanted to do things my way and I knew why fame and fortune and all the rest were just not for me.

'Felix, I don't want to send money. I want to be there – helping them, knowing them as people, touching them . . .'

'Catching leprosy and AIDS off them, no doubt!' His sneer is audible.

'You don't catch things like that!' I snap back. 'Felix, I'm grateful to you but the answer is no. I'm sure you can find a dozen other kids as good – and better – than me. I have to go now. Goodbye. And thanks again.'

I wait for his reply but all I hear is the dialling tone.

❧

'I'm sorry, Mum – really, I'm so sorry!'

My mother is standing at the kitchen sink, with tears streaming down her face.

'I didn't mean to upset you, it's just . . .' I begin.

She turns round and enfolds me in a hug.

'I'm not crying because you're giving up tennis.' She sniffs. 'I'm crying because . . . oh, I don't know . . . because I'm proud of you, I guess.'

This is news to me.

'I would never, ever have had the courage to say the things you just said,' she told me, tipping up my chin and kissing the end of my nose. 'When I was your age, I ranted and raved at my parents – but I still did what they wanted me to do.'

She smiles wryly.

'And look where it got me!' Her eyes look really sad.

'But you're going to do your own thing now, aren't you? Promise?' I plead.

I genuinely want her to be happy; but I also know that if she's busy, she won't be on my back all the time.

She nods.

'I've been thinking about it,' she says. 'I'm going to call my business 'Wall to Wall' – that covers the murals I do for kids' bedrooms, and the whole room concept as well. What do you think?'

'Ace!' I grin. 'Mum?'

'Yes?'

'You could practise on Lally's attic. I fancy something Eastern and mysterious.'

She's still waffling about pagodas and orchid-coloured ceilings when I leave for school.

'Emily Driver, I don't believe it!'

Charlie nudges me in the ribs.

'Believe what?' I mumble. My head is still spinning after my conversation with Felix, the news about Lally and how worried she is about losing her bracelet.

'You are *so* lucky!' Charlie exclaims.

I burst out laughing. 'You've been telling me that for months! What now?'

She raises her eyebrows. 'As if you didn't know!' she retorts. 'Hugo – at lunch time!'

'Oh, *that*!'

I try to sound disinterested. What he did was nice and all that, but it didn't make up for betraying my trust.

'Yes, *that*!' Charlie replies as we head towards the Science lab. 'I mean, how many guys would bring chocolates and wait at the school gates? It is so romantic!'

'It's not romantic, it's a guilty conscience!' I assure her. 'After what he did . . .'

'Oh, Emily, for heaven's sake! So he put a piece about you in the paper? So what? . . . Viki's dead chuffed.'

'Viki? What's it got to do with Viki?'

Charlie heaves a sigh.

'She took the photos, silly. And the paper is sending her a cheque. And they've said if she wants work experience she can join their photographers at the paper.'

'Cool!'

'I should warn you,' she adds, lowering her voice as we dump our bags on the table by the window, 'she's got this mad idea about asking Hugo to do another feature using loads of her pictures.'

'Oh sure – like he's really going to do that!' I try to ignore the little lurch in the pit of my stomach.

'He might,' Charlie says. 'You know the photos she took when we did community service at the old people's home? She thinks he should do a kind of "This is Your Life" feature on all the wrinklies – you know, how they go on and on about the good old days and what they did and . . .'

'That's it!'

I wheel round and give her a hug.

'That is *it*!'

Charlie gapes at me.

'What are you on about?'

'Life stories . . . old people . . . have they seen the bracelet?' My mind is racing on ahead of my words.

'Emily, you are not making any sense!'

'Wait. Stay there. If old Rawlings appears, tell him . . . oh, say I've dashed to the loo. I'll be back.'

I can see that Charlie is desperate to know what's happening but there's no time. I have to phone Hugo, and I have to do it now.

❧

Old people can be very awkward. You put yourself out to do what's best for them and what do they do? Throw it back in your face.

Hugo was up for it – in fact, he was ecstatic. I made it quite clear that I hadn't forgiven him and that he wasn't to read anything into the fact that I was speaking to him again. I wanted him to suffer. Not that he seemed to.

'It'll make an amazing feature!' he gabbled down the phone this afternoon. 'Old couple get it together after sixty years – and the bracelet thing will be the icing on the cake!'

He's on his way to Lally's house to interview her.

And now she says she won't do it.

'But Lally,' I protest, 'people all over town will read it. Someone's probably found your bracelet and when they read your story . . .'

'My story,' Lally says very quietly, 'is mine. I don't want every Tom, Dick and Harry laughing at an old woman who's still in love with a guy she sees once a year and . . .'

'Oh, Lally, they won't laugh!' I insist. 'They'll think . . .'

'No, Emily,' she repeats. 'The answer is no.'

There's the doorbell now.

Typical. Hugo's going to think I'm wasting his time and he'll probably never want to see me again. Not that I care. I mean, he deserves what's coming to him.

On the other hand . . .

Grandmothers can be so ungrateful at times.

'Well, aren't you going to let him in?' Lally asks, gesturing towards the front door.

Hugo is looking flushed and eager.

'The editor's really up for it!' he exclaims, stepping inside and waving his notebook at me. 'I'm flavour of the month – thanks to you!'

He grins at me and my stomach does the most surprising acrobatics.

'It's going to make a great story!' he adds.

'No, it's not.'

'What?' He stares at me.

'She won't do it.'

The door to the sitting room opens.

'By she, she means me!' Lally steps forward, smiling sweetly and offers Hugo her hand.

'Alice Turnbull,' she says. 'It seems my granddaughter has been leading you astray.'

Hugo shakes her hand. 'I'm sorry,' he says, 'but I don't understand. I thought you were hoping to find your lost bracelet.'

'I am,' agrees Lally, 'but I'm not prepared to have my life story splashed across the newspaper in order to do it.'

I expect Hugo to plead with her but he doesn't.

'Well,' he says thoughtfully, 'we could run an advert in the Classified section – trouble is . . .'

'That's an idea!' Lally brightens instantly.

'. . . trouble is,' Hugo goes on, 'it's not as widely read as we'd like. There is another way . . .'

'What?' Lally watches him intently.

'How would it be if I did just a small piece about you losing a bracelet given to you in the war? I mean, we do it when people lose dogs or cats – so why not bracelets?'

'Well . . .'

'I understand it has great sentimental value,' Hugo goes on. 'Would you be prepared to say why?'

'Didn't Emily tell you?' demands Lally.

Hugo shakes his head. I can't think why – I spent ages on the phone, at huge cost, telling him every last detail.

'So – you don't know the whole story?' Lally persists.

'No.' Hugo throws me a warning glance.

'Just do a piece and say that someone very dear to me gave me a shilling during the war and I had it made into a bracelet. And now it's gone.'

Hugo scribbles on his pad.

'Could you give me a bit of local colour? People do so love stories about the war – community spirit, all that stuff. Did you live in Brighton then?'

'No, London – actually, Bethnal Green. I moved to Brighton after my late husband died and my daughter got a teaching job at Deanfield School. Emily, put the kettle on, dear, while I talk to Hugo. Now, where was I? Oh yes – you see, during the war, I was working . . .'

I'll leave them to it.

I've heard it all before.

ALICE
July

The Laurels
26 Woodside Drive
Brighton

July 1st

Dearest darling Zack,

I've told them. Ruth, of course, blew a gasket but then we knew she would. Emily, bless her, thinks it's all very romantic. Today I told them we'd fixed the date! September 21st – my seventy-fifth birthday and exactly fifty-nine years from the day we first met. Emily wanted the wedding to be in Montana and was quite cheesed off when I told her we were marrying in Bethnal Green! Mega boring, I think was the phrase! But she cheered up when I said I'd buy her a new outfit for the occasion.

And now, my darling, I can confess. A couple of weeks ago, I lost the bracelet. I was devastated; I hunted high and low for it, without success, and I truly believed it was a sign and our marriage was doomed. I couldn't bear to tell you; that's why I've been so slow to write back. But it's safe! The most amazing thing happened. A charming young man, a friend of Emily's who works for our local newspaper, did a piece about it. I wasn't going to tell the whole story; but somehow, when it came to it, I couldn't lie. We've had to keep so much a secret all our lives, my darling, and now we can shout our love from the rooftops. Anyway, he printed the story and guess what? A lovely lady rang the paper to say she'd got it. Apparently, she found it on the ground by the bric-a-brac stall at the Hospital Fête and assumed that it had fallen from the stall. She was so taken with it that she bought it! Paid £2.50 she told me – £2.50 indeed! I confess I burst into tears when she handed it to me, I was so thrilled.

But there's something even more amazing – we got talking over a cup of tea and guess what? She said that her mother grew up in Bethnal Green! Well, of course, that opened the flood gates and . . . oh, it's no good, I can't string the story out any longer! Her mother was Vi.

Isn't that a coincidence? Sadly, Vi's dead now, poor lass. Cancer. Died when she was sixty-one and here's me, nearly seventy-five and about to be married to the man I love. God's been good to us, Zack. It might not have seemed like it in the past, but here we are – you with your lad and the two grandsons, and me with Ruth and Emily – and we're both in one piece.

I'll stop now, my love. Emily and Ruth are coming over to sort out a few things. To be honest, the smell of paint is getting to me but I can't say anything. They're moving in next week so we'll have a couple of months together before the wedding.

Talk to you as usual on Sunday. I say, won't we save a lot of money when these transatlantic phone calls come to an end?

I love you my darling,
Alice xxxxxx

RUTH

September

Weary with your wallpaper?
Fed up with your furnishings?
Then let

WALL TO WALL

Transform your home!

NO JOB TOO SMALL,
NO ROOM TOO DIFFICULT.

RING RUTH TURNBULL NOW
ON 01273 554109
and prepare to be amazed!

I CAN'T BELIEVE IT! Every time I open the newspaper and see the advert, I have to pinch myself. It's been more than two months now since we moved in with Ma – mind you, that hasn't been a bed of roses. To be honest, I'll be glad when the wedding's over next Saturday and Emily and I have the place to ourselves. It's funny really – I can see now that it would never have worked out – all three of us living under the same roof. Not that Ma hasn't been kind – she's helped me to kit out the conservatory with all my paint and fabric samples and she hasn't said a word when Emily blares out her music at all hours. She just flinches and sniffs a bit. Still, I know she's itching to be off with Zack and leave us to it.

He's a nice guy, Zack. To be honest, I gave him a bit of a hard time last week when we first met – quizzed him about why he wanted to marry Ma, how they would be living – I even asked about his health care policies! Well, you can't be too careful, and Ma is so naïve about the practical things in life.

I've already had three firm orders for my work and I've started on the first – a bedroom makeover for a five-year-old, whose mother clearly has more money than sense. Still, I'm not complaining!

Emily's in the Sixth Form now, of course. She played in a charity tennis match last week over in Worthing and next month she's taking part in a Sponsored Serve at Queens in London. Of course, she makes out that she's only doing it because it's in aid of Children in Need, but I'm secretly hoping that she's missing the buzz of the tennis circuit and will have a change of heart. What I haven't told her is that Felix dropped me a line and said that if all this 'adolescent nonsense' blew over, he'd be prepared to give her a second chance in the spring. I shan't say a word: I'll just wait and see what happens.

I wish Ma had been as liberal and forward thinking as I have become. Then I might have had the career I always dreamed of. Still, it's never too late, as they say. If I work flat out, I could still be famous by the time I'm sixty.

Many artists are late developers.

EMILY

June

I NEVER REALISED that A Levels were so hard. My brain feels as if it's bursting and we've hardly got going yet. It's not like it was last year; none of the teachers make allowances for me any more. I can't plead tennis coaching or post-match exhaustion as an excuse for a low grade and I can't pick Charlie's brain because she's doing different subjects.

This Economics essay is killing me; I can't get the hang of it all. Normally Lally would help – but she's not here.

I really miss her – even more than I thought I would. She's having a ball, of course. We keep getting letters about how wonderful Montana is, and how Zack's son breeds saddle horses and takes them to rodeos. She sends pictures of Zack's grandsons looking like something out of *The Horse Whisperer*, all stetsons and checked shirts and cowboy boots.

I bet they're spoiled brats.

OK, so I'm jealous. They've got Lally and I haven't.

And they will probably never, ever, have to do Economics essays.

I do hope I made the right decision. I mean, what if I fail my A Levels – what then? At least when I was playing tennis, I knew what the future held, even if I didn't much fancy it at the time. Now, all of a sudden, the future is down to me – and if I blow it, I could end up like Mum or Lally, regretting stuff for the rest of my life.

Mum's fine now, though. Her business has really taken off – so much so that my bedroom is still half decorated and the fabric I chose for my curtains is still in the John Lewis carrier bag in the box-room. Clearly I'm not a priority any more. She didn't even sympathise when I told her how hard the homework was; she just grinned and told me that hard work never hurt anyone. Call that good parenting?

But she's happy, happier than I've known her to be for ages, to be honest. She sings around the house – out of tune, but it's singing all the same; she even dresses differently, all arty and dishevelled with her hair tied up in velvet bows. She's even started seeing someone. She says there's nothing in it, but if that's the case why does she spend two hours getting ready and then practically shove me out the door to the cinema with Charlie, all expenses paid? I wasn't born yesterday.

But she's happy and that's nice.

Of course, I know what she's thinking about me. She thinks that just because I played in a couple of charity tennis matches, I'm going to pick it all up again and get back into the swing. And I'm not. Well, I don't think I am. Trouble is, I played dead well both times and raised loads of sponsorship money and the buzz was great and – oh, why can't I make up my mind?

There's the doorbell. Hugo said he'd call round; he's leaving Brighton next week because his placement at the newspaper is over and he has to go back to college. I'll miss him. I never thought I'd forgive him for what he did but to be honest, he's so fit and so sweet I couldn't stay angry for long.

I wish he didn't have to go. He says it won't make any difference to us, but it will. I know it will. He'll meet some sophisticated uni student and I'll be history.

Before I can get to the door, Mum's opened it and thrown me one of her warning glances. Honestly, I don't know what she thinks we do up here – with her creeping around the landing and constantly offering us coffee and cake, we can hardly turn my bedroom into a den of iniquity.

'Hi!' Hugo thunders up the stairs and into my room. 'How's things?'

'Foul,' I mutter. 'Why did I ever choose to do Economics? What do I care about market forces?'

'It'll be great on your CV,' he said calmly. 'Charities like that sort of thing.'

'Yes, but what if I've made the wrong decision? What if . . . ?'

'Oh, Emily, not that again – please!' He flops down on the end of my bed and kicks off his shoes. 'Can't you stop analysing everything and just get on with life?'

'Well, thanks for your support!' I burst out, knowing even as I say the words that I'm behaving like a sulky brat. 'Just because your life is all cut and dried . . .'

'Oh sure!' he retorts. 'I've taken one small step, that's all.

If I was like you, I could sit here and worry myself senseless about whether the new editor will like me, whether my copy will be good enough to make the front page, whether the pay will be enough to live on!'

He stands up and walks over to the window.

'But I'm not – I'm just taking each day as it comes and giving it my best shot and that's what you should be doing!'

I sniff.

I know he's right but I'm not going to give him the satisfaction of hearing it.

'Look at your grandmother and your mum,' he reasons, coming over and resting his hands on my shoulders as I sit at my desk. 'They made the wrong decisions with their life, right?'

I nod.

'And are they curled up in some corner, moaning?' I open my mouth to reply but he doesn't wait for me to answer. 'No they are *not* – they're making up for lost time.'

'Yes, but . . .'

He puts his fingers on my lips. It always shuts me up – I'm too busy enjoying the little shivers chasing up and down my spine to talk.

'Were your parents killed in the war? No. Is your mother refusing to let you follow your heart? No. And is your boyfriend about to disappear for half a century?'

There is a pause.

I swivel round in my chair and look up at him. 'I hope not,' I whisper.

'Me too,' he murmurs, which isn't exactly the response I want. 'But I don't know what tomorrow holds any more than you do.'

He kisses the end of my nose.

'So could we make a pact? We both give today our very best shot? If it all blows up in our faces, we'll sort it out then. OK?'

'OK,' I agree, partly because deep down I know it makes sense, but mainly because I'm hoping that a quick end to the conversation will mean the kissing can start.

It does. It's very nice.

Suddenly, I'm very much in favour of this living for the moment idea.

Very.

Also available from Piccadilly Press, by

ROSIE RUSHTON

Georgie's life is falling apart. Her mum is in a psychiatric hospital and her dad just isn't coping. No one has any idea what's going on in Georgie's head. And what's going on inside Georgie's head worries her. A lot. Her teachers say she isn't trying hard enough and her friends say she is dead weird. Georgie is pretty sure she's slowly going mad like her mum.

Then, just when she thinks she has lost it, Georgie meets Flavia Mott, a woman who at first seems even dottier than Georgie's mum. And suddenly Georgie finds herself opening up for the first time in years. But is it already too late for Georgie? Will she ever be OK again?

From the highly acclaimed author of:
The Leehampton Quartet
The Girls series
The Best Friends trilogy

Also available from Piccadilly Press, by
ROSIE RUSHTON

Who'd have thought that Chloë – cool, rich and so sophisticated – would have anything in common with Sinead, who longs for popularity?

And who'd have suspected the problems lurking beneath Jasmin's sparkling smile? And if we're talking about mysteries, then just who is Nick – the fit, supercool guy, but what is he hiding?

And what of Sanjay, who finds his computer so much more user-friendly than people? As five very different teenagers struggle to cope with their changing lives they fall into a friendship which surprises them all . . .

". . . five teenagers from very different backgrounds, the fun and drama of their lives is drawn with humour and sensitivity."
Pick of the Paperbacks – The Bookseller

If you would like more information about books available from Piccadilly Press and how to order them, please contact us at:

Piccadilly Press Ltd.
5 Castle Road
London
NW1 8PR

Tel: 020 7267 4492
Fax: 020 7267 4493

Feel free to visit our website at www.piccadillypress.co.uk